Also by Kevin Serwacki and Chris Pallace

Joey and Johnny, the Ninjas: Get Mooned

JOEY & JOHNNY THE NINJAS EPIC FAIL

Kevin Serwacki

Chris Pallace

BALZER + BRAY

An Imprint of HarperCollins*Publishers*

Balzer + Bray is an imprint of HarperCollins Publishers.

Joey and Johnny, the Ninjas: Epic Fail

Library of Congress Control Number: 2015938949
ISBN 978-0-06-229935-2

16 17 18 19 20 CG/RRDH 10 9 8 7 6 5 4 3 2 1
❖
First Edition

For Terry Pratchett and the many authors
who fostered my love of reading
—C.P.

To my grandfather, who drew me stories
that always ended with me being eaten by
something terrible, and to my grandmother,
who would make it up to me by making
me a chicken sandwich
—K.S.

JOEY AND JOHNNY
ARE DOOMED

In which Joey and Johnny are doomed.

"**J**ohnny, we are doomed!" whispered Joey.

The dooley-bopper sprouting from the top of Johnny's ninja mask shot straight up in alarm. "But that would be the third time since breakfast! Fourth, if you count breakfast itself!"

The dust of the arena curled around their feet menacingly, as if trying to drag them into the earth.

WE'RE DOOMED!

1

Dark blue thunderclouds gathered around to watch. The very air they breathed promised imminent destruction.

Together they shuffled farther out onto the arena, heroically resisting the urge to clutch each other by the arm. Headmaster FangSwan approached them, carrying a cruel-looking double-bladed instrument. It made a metallic *ching* as he held it aloft. At least the blades looked freshly sharpened, so the cut would be quick. The old man quieted the assembled crowd by flicking one eyebrow a tenth of a millimeter.

"Students," he said. The headmaster's voice hissed coldly. Several students touched their earlobes as if they could feel FangSwan's breath. "We are here to watch Pokey and Knucklebutter cut the ribbon for our new training arena. This grand reopening is a happy occasion, as you can see by these comically oversize novelty scissors! You will all clap for them."

A nervous spatter of clapping arose from the assembled crowd.

FangSwan handed the

scissors to Joey and said, "Congratulations." The word crawled out of the ancient headmaster's mouth like it had too many legs and a pair of antennae. It was a word virtually unknown to the students of Kick Foot Academy. This was sad because pretty much everything you did at KFA deserved commendation. You woke up in the morning still breathing? Congratulations! You climbed up the school's many treacherous staircases and got into a classroom without losing a limb? Congratulations! Here's a blue ribbon! You lived through the whole class? CONGRATULATIONS! Take this trophy with a cheap gold-plated ninja on it!

But there were no gold-plated trophies or festive blue ribbons at KFA. If a student deserved a pat on the back they would have to develop the flexibility to do it themselves. FangSwan would not do it for them. For FangSwan, backs were just there to be snuck up on. That's why he claimed to not actually have a back. "FangSwan has a front on both sides," he told his students. No one dared debate with him, so they had to assume it was true. Hopefully it was some sort of metaphor.

Each and every Kick Foot knew that if there was a cruel, vicious, or sarcastic way to get something done, you could be certain that FangSwan had already improved upon it. So it wasn't surprising that in spite of the grin on their headmaster's face, and the scissors that Joey now brandished uneasily, the students of KFA stood watching this ceremony with an air of deep mistrust. The question on everyone's mind was not so much "When is the other shoe going to drop?" but more "Is the shoe going to be big enough to crush us all?"

Why, you might ask, would anyone want to seek out this horrible old man? If you do ask, be sure to speak quietly so he does not hear you. The answer is simple: FangSwan is the greatest ninja master of this age. Under his guidance Kick Foot Academy had become *the* ninja school. If you wanted to be the best, you learned from FangSwan, or died trying.

Joey cleared his dry throat and addressed his fellow students: "I . . . um, declare this, uh . . . arena open?" Johnny grasped the bottom handle of the scissors while Joey held the top and together they snicked the blades through the ribbon. Half of the arena hung out over the side of the mountain, and with the ribbon gone, this half now stood open in front of them. Just a few short months ago Joey and Johnny had saved their school's honor by defeating an army of mechs. The arena was destroyed in the process, and most of it went crashing down the mountainside. FangSwan thanked them by ordering them to fix it, and that is how the boys spent their summer.

Now, it's important to note that students at Kick Foot Academy take many classes and learn thousands of useful skills, such as how to punch a shark in the teeth or how to disarm an enemy with an alligator. During all those lessons, however, they did not receive a single tip on how to rebuild a stone arena.

Like the original arena, the new one also hung out over empty space, thousands of feet off the ground. But that's where their similarities ended. This was not the rock-solid construction of the old. The arena that lay before the assembled crowd of Kick Foots had been put together by two ninjas using the power of good intentions and fairy wishes. They were ninjas, not repair guys. What the arena really needed was an architect, several stonemasons, a variety of heavy equipment, and crews to work it. Between the two of them Joey and Johnny had a sword, a hammer, and a lingering fear that today would not end well.

Like a wolf, FangSwan had a nose that could smell fear. He savored it much like a food critic might appreciate the smell of a perfectly roasted chicken. He loved to sniff the air and catch the notes of desperation. Mmmmmm, is that a tangy hint of panic? Did he detect a faint whiff of hope? Hope was an essential ingredient in producing the sweetest scented fear. Without hope, you just had despair . . . which was rather sour.

FangSwan's sniffer spoke true. An ember of hope burned inside the two boys. They were brimming with fear, and they could see failure right around the next corner. But somehow, they still had hope.

"To celebrate this arena's rebirth," the headmaster intoned, "I shall have these kittens—a symbol of new life—be the first to walk upon its virgin surface." Fang-Swan produced a box that had been hidden under his robes. He opened the lid to pathetic mews and squeaks. FangSwan stroked his long beard for effect and then reached in and pulled out one of the tiny cats.

"What did he say?" Joey asked. He and Johnny could almost see the arena sagging under the weight of their gaze. Certainly their headmaster wouldn't—

"Kitten-Mittens! No!" Johnny said as the first kitty sprinted onto the arena and then flopped to the ground to play with her paws. The others followed their sibling, causing the arena to produce a groan of strain. The gathered ninjas began to fidget uneasily.

"Gah!" Joey sputtered when a kitten Johnny had dubbed Puff-Muffin jumped onto his sister's tail. The arena issued a crisp *crack*, followed by the sound of falling pebbles. The next ball of fuzz FangSwan pulled out of the box had an adorable round belly.

"Tubby Tum-Tums!" Johnny cried.

"Stop naming them! You're only making it worse," Joey said.

"But he's the chubby one!" Everyone gasped as the kitten's clumsy frolicking was met with a rumble of settling rock and timber.

Johnny choked as Bumblekins followed Piddle-Paws followed Commander Cuddle-Fluff. There was a whole litter chasing, pouncing, and waving their paws at imaginary bugs. If not for the sound of concrete shuddering and clay tiles cracking, it would have made an extremely likable video.

Joey looked at Johnny. If the arena showed signs of collapsing—that is, *more* signs of collapsing . . . Okay. If the arena *actually* started to collapse they were going to rush out and save the kittens. Johnny looked back at Joey and nodded. It was a plan, but each boy felt a little tug of shame. If their friend Peoni had been there, she would have rushed out onto the arena five kittens ago.

Watching kittens had never been so stressful. Three Kick Foots fainted dead away when Tubby made a happy little hop, causing a racing spiderweb of cracks. By the time the last of the kittens thankfully wandered off the arena floor, beads of sweat had broken out on the face of every student. The remaining members of

the audience who weren't unconscious let out a stuttering sigh of relief.

Yes, the arena had successfully held up to the pressures of thumping tails and pouncing paws. FangSwan clapped his hands together and said, "We are now ready to do our morning exercises."

There was a collective *schloorp* sound as everyone simultaneously retracted their sighs of relief.

"Ladies first," FangSwan said.

The girls shuffled forward, giving Joey and Johnny a look that made it clear that if KFA ever had a prom, Joey and Johnny would be going with each other. Mai-Fan, being one of the smaller girls, delicately put her toe out before stepping onto the visibly crumbling arena. Joey cast his eyes to the ground while Johnny waved and gave the girls an encouraging gesture with his thumbs. Gestures were returned to Johnny, but they weren't encouraging and they used other fingers.

FuShoe leaned close as she passed Joey and hissed in his ear, "I'm going to take the time we spend falling to punch you repeatedly in the face."

By this time it was getting difficult to hear FangSwan over the continuous shower of snapping concrete. The headmaster made a little flick with his fingers, making it clear that the rest of the students were to proceed to their doom. They did so dutifully.

"At least the kittens are safe," Johnny said, adding

his weight to the arena. Still standing on solid ground, FangSwan began to lead them all in a rousing set of jumping jacks.

This was it, then. The end. Killed by shoddy workmanship. Joey took a deep breath and looked skyward, hoping that the old ninja masters might send them salvation. Instead, he found the word that saved them all.

That word was "DRAGON!"

PIRATES

In which we talk about something
completely different.

"**A**rrrrrr!" said the pirate.

WISEMAN NOTE: Yes, this is the
ONLY way to begin a chapter on pirates.

"Arrrrr?" he said again when the first "arrrrr" was
ignored.

The pirate captain wearily looked up from the book
he was jotting notes in. "Yes, Captain First Mate, what
can I do for you?"

Captain First Mate eagerly stepped forward and
gave a salute that looked as though he'd just made it
up on the fly. He'd yet to discover a salute that looked

piratey enough. This is possibly because pirates don't salute. "Aye, Cap'n Captain! Captain Lookout sez he saws a boat offin thar starboard side!"

Cornelius Loon, otherwise known as Captain Captain, had to concentrate through a headachy fog to piece together what had just been said to him. The man's pirate accent was thicker today.

"Was it to the left or right, Captain First Mate?"

"Arrrr? It was tar the left, Cap'n Captain!"

Cornelius rubbed his throbbing temples. "Then that would be 'port,' Captain First Mate. Just stick with right and left, would you?"

He'd said this countless times to his new officers, but it had never taken. Cornelius had no explanation for the mystery of the pirate accent. His crew was a mash-up of all sorts, from every walk of life you could imagine. He had ex–car mechanics from Jersey, lawyers from Spain, and a shoe salesman from the Congo. His newest recruit was a gentleman named Chadford Pennyworthington. He was an aging professor with an advanced degree in prehistoric English gardening. Before joining up he spoke as though politely arguing a point that everyone already agreed upon. After just five minutes on the ship he was telling his fellow crew members to "Git thar barnacle-blistered backsides over the mizzenmast and untie the yardarm!"

It would have been okay if they actually used the

proper nautical terms, but most of the time they were just trying to sound more piratey. Their lookout, Captain Lookout, had the habit of always saying things were on the starboard side of the ship. This was because the word "starboard" sounded cooler. So Cornelius knew that on any given day there was only a 50 percent chance that their lookout was giving them the right directions.

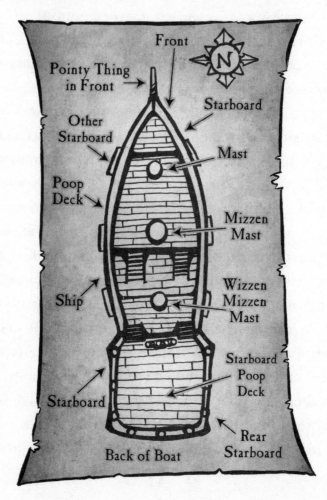

When Cornelius had taken command, he—like many captains before him—made certain changes in the roster. Namely, he got rid of any officers or go-getters who were overly loyal to the previous captain. She had been a rather impressive captain, so Cornelius decided to clean house. Despite their faults, his new officers were intelligent men. They certainly were not shipshape yet, but they'd come around in time . . . he hoped.

Fortunately, Cornelius didn't really need them for the day-to-day running of the ship. For that there were the veterans. At the core of any pirate ship lies a group of brutish, bloodthirsty brigands. Men with arms that look like carved pieces of wood, and legs that are, in fact, carved pieces of wood. These men didn't care that there was a new captain; most of them didn't even notice. They just waited to be told what to hit and when. The only thing they knew was pirating. The veterans maintained the ship, flowing through it like blood through your body. And like blood, it was a hor-rible thing when they came spilling out.

Cornelius was smart enough to know he needed them, but that didn't make them any less terrifying.

And then there was the "Captain" thing. This was a part of their history, but it didn't make it any less headache-inducing. It was all thanks to a rousing hundred-year-old speech.

Much has been said about how much ninjas and pirates hate each other. It's sort of true, in that they've heard of each other and they don't like what they've heard, but they're not really at war. They don't have time to be at war with each other because they are both far too busy fighting with their own kind. One ninja clan is always trying to wipe out another, and this is true for pirates as well.

You see, superheroes have it easy: they have a nice, simple, clearly defined class of enemy known as *supervillains*. This means superheroes can have barbecues with one another and borrow each other's utility belts without any trouble. They *know* who the enemy is. Pirates and ninjas don't have that, so they form rival clans or rival schools or rival boats and do battle with their own kind.

The rousing speech in question was the result of one of these pirate battles. The Loons, named after their captain, Frederick Loon, were losing to the Bearded Tigers. The Tigers had more ships, more men, and better cannons. The Loons just had a captain who was really good at speeches. When all seemed lost he climbed the mainmast of his burning ship and bellowed what would be forever known as the Captains

Speech. Frederick Loon declared that they were all in it together. That this was their ship, their fight, and that today every member of his fleet, from the deck scrubber to the first mate, was a captain! A captain of his own destiny! "WE! ARE ALL! CAPTAINS!" His words were met with a mighty roar of approval that made the sails billow.

It worked. The tide of battle turned spectacularly as even the lowliest of the Loons, filled to bursting with pride and self-importance, fought back with the strength of a hundred pirate captains.

Afterward, Frederick had to reestablish that although they were all captains, he was the captain captain, and that meant they still had to listen to him. But the title alone made his men feel better and elevated the Loons' spirits to the very top spot in the pirate hierarchy.

Cornelius spent at least a portion of every single day cursing that speech. He had tried to keep it from his new officers, but the veterans passed it on to them like a disease.

Captain First Mate stood shuffling his feet, obviously waiting for something. Cornelius couldn't even remember why the man was there . . . oh, wait! A ship!

"So, arrr? Should we turn hard to starboard and get the ship, Cap'n?"

"No," replied Cornelius, slapping papers off his desk as he searched for his bottle of aspirin. "We should turn to the *left* and get the ship!"

They took the ship in three minutes. This was a record, so the crew exchanged hearty "Arrrrs" and clinked their swords together in celebration. It was the only use they had for their swords, since there was not the slightest bit of resistance to be had.

Cornelius never trusted the easy captures, particularly this one, since the owner of the ship greeted him on deck with a handshake and an unexpected, "I was expecting you, Captain Loon."

No one *expected* a pirate! That was the whole point! If they had expected pirates they would've gone a different way. Cornelius had sixty men covering a yacht that appeared to be empty, save for this one fellow. So why did Captain Captain feel outnumbered?

"I'm afraid, sir, that I don't know your name in return," he said, shaking the offered hand and looking around for a trap. The man had offered his left hand—something looked off about the right one. Honestly, something was off about the left one too, but the right one was worse. Pirates were no strangers to prosthetic limbs, but still . . .

"Scar EyeFace, at your service," the man said, "and it's no trap, Captain. I wanted to speak with you. I have a proposition that will profit us both."

The pirate captain looked at the ship, which was clearly expensive and filled with equipment that even he couldn't identify. "You've got my ear, sir, but your ship still belongs to me."

"Of course!" said the man, with the air of someone who had just dropped a penny and couldn't be bothered to pick it up again. "Consider it payment for considering my proposal. Basically, I want you to crash a party."

While the man explained the details, Cornelius tried to study the fellow. His face was impossible to read. The long scar running through his left eye gave

it a look of constant malice. Despite his rather tacky
Hawaiian shirt, he was certainly no overfed tourist.
He had the body language of an expert politician;
every gesture looked practiced and polished. No information was being given away that wasn't expressly
intended.

And the thing he wanted. You don't hire pirates
to crash a party—just tell them where it is and they'll
crash it on their own. And you certainly don't travel
all the way from Lemming Falls to Badoni Dony to
ask them. This was obviously a trap, and Cornelius
was clever enough not to walk into it. He didn't even
want the yacht anymore, but then the scarred man

said something that changed Cornelius's mind. It was the payment for their services—specifically, the Great Tooth and how to be rid of it.

"I don't know exactly where the party is, so I'm going to have to send you to school," said the scarred man.

"A school?" asked Cornelius. "What kind of school?"

Scar EyeFace told him.

"Really!" said the pirate captain in surprise. "They have schools for *that*?"

A NINJA BARBECUE

In which everything is
really, *really* well done.

"**J**ohnny! It's a dragon! It's perfect!" cried Joey.

"I know!" said Johnny with equal enthusiasm. "'Burned to a pile of ash' is going to sound so much better than 'fell off a mountain'!"

Flames jetted toward the scattering Kick Foots. The beast was sixty feet long with poison-green stripes twisting about its black armored body. The wind billowing from its beating wings knocked stone statues from their pedestals and sent students sprawling into the dust. Hungry tendrils of fire engulfed a nearby equipment shed, making it explode in a shower of stone and broken weapons. FangSwan frowned in annoyance, and that is what truly worried Joey.

"No," said Joey, ducking under a fireball, "if we get the dragon to destroy the arena, FangSwan won't be able to blame us!"

Johnny decided to not mention FangSwan's history of assigning blame to whoever he liked regardless of actual guilt. The old man had once blamed a student for a cloud formation he didn't find pleasing. Expecting the headmaster to be fair was like asking a forest fire to be reasonable. However, Johnny didn't have a plan beyond checking wind direction to see where his ashes would end up. Joey's plan was marginally better.

"Okay," said Joey, using a broken spear to vault over a flaming wall. "One of us has to distract FangSwan while the other one runs onto the crumbling arena and provokes that monster into destroying the evidence of our shoddy workmanship!"

"Great plan!" said Johnny. "I'll take the dragon!"

"Coward!" shouted Joey. He veered toward Fang-Swan and tried to think of something that would take the man's attention away from the screeching, giant reptile spewing jets of flame at his school. Maybe a joke? Some juggling? There was only one thing Joey could think of, but using it would risk unleashing an even more savage monster than the one currently attacking them.

FangSwan stood with his hands clasped behind his back, watching the scene of devastation at his feet. He wouldn't have admitted this to anyone, but he liked dragons. Nearly immortal, scaly monsters with the heart of a volcano. Cruel beasts who'd snap a man up in their toothy jaws without a second thought. They reminded him of himself, when he'd been young and soft.

This dragon was also giving his students a valuable and amusing lesson in dodging firebolts. Perhaps he could offer the dragon a full-time teaching job. The ancient headmaster was pondering a classroom made entirely out of lava when one of his students hesitantly approached him. Lips tightening, FangSwan wondered if it was the idiot, the nitwit, the simpleton, or the twit.

Joey started with "Um . . . uh . . ."

It was the nitwit. FangSwan turned the full force of his gaze on his student, making Joey stumble to his knees. "Stop making confused mouth-hole noises and speak."

"Headmaster, I saw something that you should know about!" Joey blurted.

"Are you going to tell me about the dragon? I saw it. Do not expect extra credit for this."

"No, headmaster." A ball of fire punctuated this remark by exploding just above their heads. Joey dropped to the ground and slapped his arms about, trying to put out the embers. FangSwan didn't move at all, his focus continuing to invisibly pummel Joey. "I . . . I found something worse."

FangSwan's eyebrow silently asked the obvious question.

"It's Flippy the Ninja, sir," replied Joey. At the sound of the name, FangSwan's toes cracked the stone beneath his feet.

Flippy the Ninja was the brainchild of Carl

Crescent. Last year Carl had created a rival ninja school, Red Moon Academy. It failed spectacularly, but even as Carl slunk away in humiliating defeat, Flippy remained, and leapt to the top of FangSwan's list of sworn enemies.

It would be impossible to compile a complete list of FangSwan's enemies. Part of the reason was that there were actually two lists. The first contained the usual assortment of rival ninja clans and lone warriors who had exhausted all other tests of bravery and self-destruction. Despite their desire to cause the headmaster (and sometimes his students) bodily harm, FangSwan couldn't truly hate them. Which was strange considering the ease with which he hated things. But in fact, FangSwan was never happier than when he was battling a truly competent and dangerous foe. They were the only people who got to see him in a good mood—albeit not for long.

The second list contained the poor saps who had no idea they'd made the list in the first place. Every clerk who ever told him to "have a nice day," or the woman who asked him if he had any grandchildren, or the interior designer who came to his school and used the phrase "breakfast nook."

In many ways, it was more dangerous to be in the second category. He did not see them as *his* enemies: he saw them as enemies of everything ninja, worms tunneling through the bedrock of ninja's ancient and honorable name. They were the things that made his students cuddly and weak, and Flippy was their king.

The spunky, eye-catching mascot for Red Moon was on a forest of billboards, TwitFace ad campaigns, and comic books. Worse, Flippy had entered the public mind. He was printed on ironic T-shirts and sprayed as graffiti. Flippy was every cupcake, sappy song, boy band, decaffeinated latte, and wearable blanket that FangSwan despised. All crafted into the shape of a chubby little ninja.

At first their headmaster had been so enraged by the concept that he had lashed out. The billboards were the first to go, smashed into kindling so fine it could've been used as toothpicks for termites. It was sometime on the third day of his wrath, as FangSwan punched through a poster of Flippy—and the wall behind it—when he came to a realization. He was having . . . there's a word for it . . . *fun*. Flippy the Ninja wasn't alive. Nor was he strictly physical. He was not going to be like any other adversary FangSwan had ever fought. Flippy was an idea.

And FangSwan had never killed an idea before.

"You have my attention," FangSwan said.

While the dragon was busy spraying fire at everyone else, Johnny was thinking about a book he'd read as a boy. It was written by a native of his home island, Badoni Dony, a woman named Arugalla Picklebee. She had gone completely insane and had no idea she was now writing award-winning children's books. The particular book Johnny had in mind was titled *Brucy the Inedible Brussels Sprout*. The hero of the book, Brucy, struggled to fulfill his fondest wish, which was to be eaten by a hungry child. Alas, this was unlikely because Brucy was a brussels sprout and brussels sprouts are totally gross.

After many failed attempts Brucy was eventually taken in by a kindly old woman. She introduced him to Billy Bacon-Bits, with whom he had a short-lived but rewarding friendship. Using teamwork they were both devoured by hungry orphans.

WISEMAN NOTE: This book won the Booker T. Fellows award for "Most Awkwardly Happy Ending."

Johnny had never felt closer to Brucy than he did right now. His only mission was to be attacked by an angry dragon. A feat that should have been no trouble at all, but was, for some reason, seemingly impossible. The dragon just wasn't having it. He was perfectly happy belching explosive air at the other students, but not so much as a lick of flame came anywhere near Johnny. It was making him feel self-conscious.

Out of desperation, Johnny yelled Brucy's catchphrase, "EVERYONE CAN BE DELICIOUS! EVEN A BRUSSELS SPROUT!"

"Johnny? Did you just tell that dragon you're delicious? I'm pretty sure it already knows that."

Johnny spun to find Peoni staring at him with one expertly arched eyebrow.

"PEONI! Where have you been?"

She gave him the same blank look that he and Joey had been getting from her all summer. Peoni buttoned her top lip with her lower and that was that.

"Fine!" said Johnny. "Then I'm not going to tell you why I'm trying to get this dragon to eat me!"

"You're not trying to get the dragon to eat you! You're trying to get him to destroy that death trap you and Joey spent the summer building!"

"Uh-h-h," Johnny stalled.

"And that dragon is never going to attack you while you're covered in kittens!"

As lances of flame shot down from the sky, Johnny had saved the kittens. Flipping and bobbing and weaving through the chaos, Johnny had scooped up each ball of fluff from the melee. Even now he stood with their box tucked under one arm.

"No self-respecting dragon is going to roast a kitten!"

WISEMAN NOTE: This is entirely true. A dragon-fighting knight made this discovery in the early fourteenth century. He found that dragon slaying became incredibly easy once he donned his suit of live kitten armor. The hard part was living with the name "Sir Pussy-Cat."

"Okay, Johnny, I'm going to get these guys out of here," Peoni said. "The second I'm gone, that dragon is going to be gunning for you. Got it?"

"Peoni?" said Johnny.

"What?"

"You're my Billy Bacon-Bits!"

Peoni blushed for a moment. "You shouldn't read that woman's books, Johnny, you're weird enough without them." With that, she slung the box under her arm and dashed through the panicked crowd of fellow Kick Foots.

There was a thump as the dragon landed on solid ground and its scaly, horned head turned to face the now kittenless Johnny. Twin jets of steam snorted from cavernous nostrils and the dragon swallowed in expectation. Of all the ninjas here, only this one kept insisting that he was delicious. To be honest, Johnny felt relieved. It's no fun to feel unwanted. In the green glint of the monstrous beast's eyes, there was the unmistakable look of desire. A desire to see him burn.

Johnny pulled his hammer from nowhere just in time to block the gout of fire that burst from the dragon's toothy jaws. A reptilian smile bared saber-long teeth as its prey backed slowly into the arena. Spinning the wooden mallet to put out the flames, Johnny prepared himself for the next attack. The dragon walked forward, chest puffed full of molten air, mouth open wide, like an opera singer holding a long note. The force of the blast actually drove Johnny backward, and he was certain his dooley-bopper was now on fire. He had reached the middle of the arena, the point at which the mountain fell away. Johnny was now supported only by the work he and Joey had done all summer. The thought of it made him sweat.

The dragon continued to spew smaller flaming spitballs at Johnny, forcing him closer to the outer edge. Johnny managed to knock them aside with his ever-spinning hammer, but this was not something he could keep up for long. Some of his fellow students had taken position on smoldering rooftops. A few had even acquired bows, their arrows bouncing harmlessly off the dragon's armored plates.

Four more steps and Johnny could go no farther. He could feel the stones shifting under his feet. One dropped clear away, creating a preview of his immediate future. The dragon sensed his distraction. Johnny looked up as the great beast pounced, and in a moment of clarity he noticed it was not entirely unlike a kitten.

"Show me," FangSwan demanded.

Joey was trying to think where he could find a Flippy the Ninja, but nothing was happening. He had successfully led their headmaster away from the arena, taking shelter between two of the school's buildings, but there was no time to go looking. It was pointless at any rate—FangSwan had already destroyed everything with an image of Flippy in a nine-mile radius.

Almost everything.

"Where is this Flippy, boy?"

Joey was looking at the headmaster's eyes as he spoke. He was fairly certain that for a brief moment the glints of light in them changed to skulls. There was no other choice—Joey reached inside his uniform and pulled out a much-folded and worn piece of paper. FangSwan snatched it from the boy's hands.

Intentionally or not, their friend Ting had gone undercover at the Red Moon Academy. This had led to many things, including Ting becoming Red Moon's champion; the disappearance and possible disintegration of Joey's rival, Brad; and Ting leaving on a quest of redemption. It had been a busy year.

On the day he disappeared from Kick Foot, the only thing Ting had left behind was a drawing of Flippy. The drawing had made Joey first furious, and then sad. In time it became a symbol of his missing friend and he looked at it often. If there had been any other way to distract his headmaster he would have taken it.

"This is not Flippy," FangSwan said. "It appears to be a starfish with an Aqua-Lung." Ting was not the world's greatest artist.

Seeing the terrified look on Joey's face, FangSwan

added, "You were right to bring it to me. You can never be too sure."

"Oh. *Oh*, thank you, headmaster. Can I . . ." Fang-Swan threw the drawing into one of the many piles of burning debris. Joey watched it curl and smoke.

There was a thunderous crash.

WISEMAN NOTE: No, that was not nearly loud enough. That should have been written: There was a THUNDEROUS CRASH!

FangSwan headed in the direction of the sound and Joey followed him. The arena was a smoldering ruin, its remains once again strewn at the foot of the great mountain. Through the smoke, Joey could just spot a pair of fingers gripping the torn, blackened edge where the arena had fallen away. He ran over to help Johnny up.

"Thanks, Joey," Johnny said, extinguishing his dooley-bopper. "You should have seen it! He leapt! I leapt—only half a second later, so that when the dragon's weight snapped the arena in two I ran up his body as he fell. When I got to the end of his tail, I hurled myself into space. Almost didn't make it!" Johnny let out a long breath. "Still, one big BOOM—two problems solved."

"Super ninja, Johnny," Joey said, "but you mean— *one* problem solved."

"What?"

"You do know that dragons can fly, right?"

That's when another call rang out across the mountain: "THERE'S A SECOND DRAGON!"

The dragon Johnny had been fighting was simply surprised by the arena dropping out beneath him. Nothing more. Since then he had flown up to join a second, larger dragon. They seemed to be having a meeting. When a decision had been made, they flew down to land. The ragged Kick Foots banded together, crouching in various fighting stances as they prepared for the next wave of attacks.

But the dragons alighted gently on the ground like butterflies and bowed their necks. All were keen to note that the larger dragon had a rider on his back. The man was tall and armored in a suit of green scales. He slid off his mount, smoothly landing on the ground with a soft clank. The helmeted warrior stood, calmly looking at the ring of ninjas around

him. There was no noise except the crackling of a few fires. The Kick Foots were holding their breath. The dragon rider reached up and pulled his helmet off, letting his flowing blond locks catch in the wind. "Hey, fellas! Sorry about the arena. Maybe I can help rebuild it?"

Brad had returned. He wasn't dead, or disintegrated, or on the moon. He was back and he didn't even have the decency to have helmet hair.

Several of the female students swooned at the sight of him. In a blink he was surrounded by a crowd of well-wishers and welcome-back-ers. Hugs were given. Tears were shed. Even Fang-Swan came forward to shake the boy's hand.

Joey clenched his fists. "Braaaad!" he growled, but he managed to do it very quietly.

Peoni bent her head to Johnny and whispered, "Oh, man. Who's going to tell Ting?"

4

LETTERS FROM TING

In which, sadly,
Ting does his very best.

Hi, guys and Peoni,

You're probably wondering what happened. Why I left again. Brad saved me. He saved me and I refuse to believe he died doing it. So I've decided to save him right back! I believe that he's out there somewhere, and I'm going to find him. Wish me luck.

Weird thing is, I talked with my mom about it and she was surprisingly cool. She said my dad also went on a quest of discovery when he was younger. Only he was going out to find himself... which seems dumb. Anyway, he runs a movie theater now. I guess after having a bunch of adventures on his own he discovered that he'd rather watch other people have them instead. Huh.

Well, I better wrap this up. Brad ain't gonna find himself.

Your friend,
TING

lone wolf, finder of Brad

p.s. Red Moon was kinda lame, but they had the right idea with the titles. I kinda miss being the Guardian of the North Wind.

Hi, guys and Peoni,

Cold and out of food. Night is approaching and the wind is starting to pick up. I can barely see the sign that says: "Lemming Falls—Five Miles." Five miles in two days? Not bad.

Oh, I met a dog. He's a mutt, some kind of beagle mix. He's got an explorer's heart, and we have bonded in that way that only lone wolf adventurer types can. I have to admit that I don't have a solid plan for what to do next, so I'm going

to trust my gut. Armed with my lucky compass, my loyal companion, and my unbending will, nothing can stop us. Next stop: Brad.

UPDATE: No longer hungry. My mom drove a care package out to me and it had my favorite fruity throwing stars ("Frutars, made with real fruit colors!") and some soup. Finder ate all the beef jerky, though. She also said that she'd mail this letter. Thanks, Mom!

Your friend,
TING
wolf-pack pilgrim

Hi, guys and Peoni,
My gut told me to head east, so we left the main road and walked into the wild. One problem: About an hour later I dropped my compass and Finder ate it. I don't think it's coming back out. Not sure I'd use it if it did. Sounds bad, I know, but ever since the "incident" he's been extra determined. Really seems to know where he's going. I think maybe the compass gave him super-direction powers. Wouldn't be the weirdest origin story. The Fiddler was left on a

38

beach as a baby and raised by crabs. Silly, maybe, but that doesn't protect criminals from his sideways-scuttling fury.

This might be exactly the break I needed! Lead on, brave Finder!

Your friend,

TING

dog follower

p.s. I know what you're thinking, but even if my dog does have superpowers that doesn't make me his sidekick. So stop snickering.

p.p.s. No offense, Knight-Lite.

Hey, guys and Peoni,

Disaster! After a day and a half, Finder and I stumbled out of the woods onto another road. Shortly thereafter a car pulled up and Finder's owners stepped out. Mr. and Mrs. Yawnwick were so grateful they were almost crying. I can only hope I will feel as good when I find Brad.

Turns out his name is Mr. YumYum (yuck) and he has a terrible sense of direction. They said he often gets lost trying to find his way to the house from the backyard. I gave a solemn good-bye to Finder (I refuse to call him Mr.

YumYum) and accepted his owners' heartfelt thanks.

The Yawnwicks offered me a ride home, but when I told them of my quest they seemed impressed and gave me an old jacket from their trunk, an LED headlamp, two Pizza Logs, and a combo meal from MacFrugal's Hamburg Shack. They also said they'd post these last two letters. Hope you get them soon.

It's probably for the best that Finder and I bumped into them. They pointed out that we were on the same highway we left two days ago and we were heading back toward Lemming Falls.

Your friend,

TING

lone(ly) wolf

p.s. Finder did manage to pass the compass, but I decided I don't really need it anymore.

Hey, guys and Peoni,
I have no idea where I am,
or how to get back. Shoulda
kept that poop compass.
TING
lost wanderer of the
somewhere

5

BRAD IS SO AWESOME

In which Brad is . . . aw man,
he's just such a great guy!

Joey, Johnny, and Peoni stood together next to the still-smoking remains of the arena. Peoni had her hand in the box of kittens and would occasionally utter a soft curse and pull her hand free saying, "Aah! Don't bite!" after which she'd put her hand right back in the box.

The ninja friends were nearly invisible, but not from their years of stealth training. They were unseen because the crowd only had eyes for Brad. He looked no worse for his unexpected journey. Actually, he looked better . . . taller? He smiled and greeted his adoring throng, finding a moment and a kind word for each of them.

FangSwan glowed with a mysterious emotion that none of his students could identify. It seemed like a distant relation to "content," like happy's mean cousin. The "celebration" "honoring" Joey and Johnny for "rebuilding" the arena had turned into a *celebration* for Brad. There were even banners—big ones—welcoming him back. Some of them were still wet. Joey knew in his heart that everything about their grand reopening ceremony had been a mockery, but it still fueled his jealous flames.

"We didn't get banners," Joey grumped.

"It's great that Brad's back," declared Johnny, "but there's still dragons to fight!"

No, there weren't. The two dragons had joined the party and were chatting amiably to a small crowd of curious Kick Foots. The larger lizard was the dragon king, the smaller, his envoy.

FuShoe was standing as close to the immense dragon as he would allow. It took all of her self-control to keep from hugging him and begging him to stay. She settled for gazing at him adoringly as he spoke.

And it wasn't enough that Brad rode home on a

dragon—*they were indebted to him*. After being tele-ported to the other side of the planet, Brad met, befriended, and performed some great service to the Dragons of the East, thus earning their eternal loyalty. Brad was too modest to allow the story to be told, so they were spared the exact details. Lucky, really, for the dragon king's voice rang over the mountainside in a thunderous bass. Every time he spoke, more debris fell from the sundered arena. A retelling of the tale might have brought down the whole school.

"I TOLD THIS YOUNG ONE TO GO FORTH AND ALERT YOU TO MY ARRIVAL," said the dragon king.

The dragon envoy hung his head sheepishly and clawed the ground in embarrassment. "They were well alerted, my master!"

"THESE ARE FRIENDS OF THE GREAT AND GLORIOUS BRAD! I MEANT BRING THEM A CAKE OR DO THE DANCE OF GREETING!"

The dragon king attempted to whisper to FuShoe, "I'M SORRY ABOUT HIM, HE'S NEW." When her ears stopped ringing, FuShoe nodded sympathetically. Then the dragon king reared to address the whole school: "FRIENDS OF THE MAGNIFICENT BRAD! I AM TRULY SORRY ABOUT THE DESTRUCTION OF YOUR POORLY BUILT ARENA!"

"Hey! That's not fair!" muttered Joey.

WISEMAN NOTE: It was totally fair.

"WORRY NOT! WE SHALL BUILD IT ANEW! JUST GIVE US ABOUT AN HOUR."

The two dragons lifted themselves into the air with a flapping of wings that knocked the crowd of Kick Foots onto their butts. The great reptiles were true to their word. They immediately busied themselves gathering boulders, chunks of iron ore, and mighty tree trunks. With careful blasts of their molten breath they fused stone, wood, and steel. The resulting construction was a masterpiece of dragon architecture that could take one's breath away. They even included a glistening statue of Brad standing with his hands on his hips and casting a heroic gaze over the bright horizon.

When the dragons were done, they bowed low to Brad, who gave each of their long faces a friendly hug. The dragon king made his final speech.

"FAREWELL, LUCKY FOLLOWERS OF BRAD THE STUPENDOUS! IF YOU SHOULD EVER REQUIRE HELP FROM ME, KING OF DRAGONS, SIMPLY HOLD ALOFT THE HORN OF GLAVENSGILL AND SAY THE WORDS OF . . ."

FangSwan stepped forward midspeech and waved his hand at the dragon.

"AH. WELL . . . UH, GOOD-BYE THEN . . . ," said the dragon king as he flew off with his envoy following close behind. The students watched as the two faded into the distance.

"Dragon and fairy time is done," said FangSwan, snapping them back to *his* reality. "Go to class."

GETTING BEAT UP
BY MONSTERS

In which everyone is painfully clobbered.
Sensitive people should skip ahead.

The next day Joey walked through the busy quad when something caught his eye. Overnight Fang-Swan had reworked the student assessments and posted a declaration that Brad was ranked first in all classes.

"But he just got here!" Joey blurted before realizing that FangSwan was within earshot.

The headmaster rounded on Joey, pointing a long, bony finger at him. "You! Do something ninja-y!"

"Uh, I . . . wha?" stammered Joey.

"Do not make me repeat myself."

"Yes, sir!" said Joey, whipping his sword around while flipping backward. By the time he landed, the sword was back in his scabbard. In front of Joey, a speck of ash split into five separate pieces.

"Nice going!" said Brad, who was standing nearby. "And I thought you were good when I left."

FangSwan pointed at Brad. "Do it better."

Brad looked apologetically at Joey and did as he was asked. He flipped, his sword flashed, and another piece of ash floated in five separate directions. Nothing was done any differently, but . . . there was just a special something . . . something undeniably better.

FangSwan grunted in satisfaction and stalked away, leaving Joey clenching his fists. Brad looked embarrassed, but had the good sense to let it drop.

Johnny clapped his friend on the shoulder. "Man, Brad's GOOD! Come on, let's go see Sensei Kendu. I bet punching something will cheer you up."

Fight Class

Kendu's classroom was as unkempt as ever. Teetering stacks of boxes, dressers, and chests lined the walls of the roughly rounded room. In the center was a huge cube draped with a thick burgundy cloth. Some of the students who arrived early were tempted to take a peek beneath the fabric, but quickly changed their minds when the cloth billowed out a gust of swampy air and emitted a clicking gibber that shook the boards under their feet.

Still, it was better than the time there had been nothing at all. Generally, fight class was wonderfully straightforward. You were either presented with something to fight, or something to fight with. The class had grown accustomed to facing horrors, or waking up in the nurse's office, or both. Somehow facing *nothing* had been worse.

That day Kendu had been uncommonly still. Long, feathered arms folded neatly across her chest, her lean form waiting next to the door the students had just entered. Any question was met with her strange bird-smile and a simple gesture toward the center of the room. Eventually Whistler, a lanky ninja with pointy elbows, wondered aloud if maybe it—whatever it was— was invisible.

One by one the Kick Foots began to feel their way in search of a translucent catapult, or a kickboxing hobbit. Soon the entire class was climbing over one another feeling about for that day's lesson. Johnny had just suggested that maybe it was invisible *and* intangible when there was a distinctive and unsettling *click*.

"Fight!" Kendu said in a perfect mimicry of a human voice.

The floor was suddenly gone, and nine-point-eight meters per second later, the entire class lay in a bruised and twisted pile of limbs thirty feet down.

"Sensei," Joey complained, "I don't think we can fight gravity."

Say what you want, Sensei Kendu kept you on your toes. With her at the helm, there was more to fighting than monsters and melee. Which brings us back to today and what was inside the box.

"What do you think it is, Johnny?" asked Joey.

"Maybe we have to fight our own imaginations," Johnny said, staring at the covered cube.

Joey had long since learned to roll with Johnny's thought process. "Explain," he said.

"Maybe whatever's under there is exactly as horrible as we think it is. If we imagine it's the worst thing ever, it will be. Picture an indestructible killing machine, and it is."

Joey slid Johnny a glance. "You're thinking about RabbitShark, aren't you?"

"No . . . ," Johnny said, "but I am now!" He smiled widely.

"Based on your theory, shouldn't we all focus our thoughts on an adorable baby piglet?"

"We should," Johnny admitted, "but now I want to see RabbitShark!"

"You better hope you're wrong," Joey said.

When the burgundy curtain was lifted, it was a testament to the bravery of Sensei Kendu's students that only two of them fainted. Half of them jumped backward, and many looked toward the exits. Only Johnny made a little "awww" of disappointment.

The creature inside the box was not RabbitShark. It was a perfect fusion of jellyfish and spider. Its body rose on clicking segmented legs and slime-covered tentacles, filling most of the ten-foot cage that contained it. Where the creature wasn't covered with chitinous armor, its body was gelatinous. If this thing had crawled out of anyone's imagination, they were watching the wrong kind of movies.

WISEMAN NOTE: The creature in question is an Arachnidarian, and a rather healthy one at that. Specifically, the Goliath Nettle Box Widow, whose Latin name is . . . well, I think we both know you're not really going to read the Latin, are you? You're going to look at it and say "long Latiny name" and move on, so I'm not going to bother writing it down and we'll call ourselves even. Okay? For the record, I could spell it if I had to.

Kendu's perfect voice said, "Fight." Feathered fingers pulled a rope, which slid a pin from the top of the cage. For a moment, nothing happened, but then the barred walls fell to the ground with a metal *clang*. The creature spun to face the ninjas surrounding it. Two of

its spider legs rhythmically rubbed themselves in front of its unspeakable mouth. They rasped and sloshed at the same time. The sound made Joey feel a bit queasy.

The Kick Foots readied themselves more, if that was even possible. Many of them tried to circle the beast for a better angle of attack. This proved to be somewhat difficult to accomplish due to its many eyes and its ability to redistribute them inside its semisolid form.

"Eeeww!" cried FuShoe.

"BLEUUUUUUuU-UUuuu . . . ," burbled the beast. The tension grew thick.

"Fight!" Kendu repeated, a little more insistently. Normally by now someone was unconscious.

The Arachnidarian's lower body pulsed and twisted, matching the pace of the circling students. Its upper body remained still, now with four great spider legs raised and ready to lash out.

There is honor in landing the first blow, but without learning more of the creature's strengths and weaknesses such an *honor* would be dubious at best. Who cares about landing the first blow? Ninjas would rather make sure they were still around to deliver the last one.

"Joey, I'm going for it," Johnny said, trying to keep his voice steady.

Johnny drew his hammer from wherever he kept it. The beast countered by whipping two tentacles around Spratt and wielding him like a club. Johnny crouched, ready to leap into the air with a move he called "the

Hammerhead" . . . which was fairly self-explanatory.

"Wait!" cried Joey. He grabbed the back of the hammer and urged Johnny to set it on the ground. Spratt was likewise dropped to the floor, albeit less daintily. "Everyone, put down your weapons."

Slowly everyone lowered and then placed their weapons down. The monster's eyes swiveled about before it, too, relaxed its horrible spider legs and tentacles. It swayed very slowly from side to side, emitting a strange gurgling bubble.

"I think it's friendly?" said someone.

"Its burbling almost sounds like a cat's purr."

"It's making my teeth itch."

A dull blue luminescence began deep inside its gooey flesh, and soon the Arachnidarian's form was glowing, gently passing through a series of blues and greens. The purring continued; if anything, it grew stronger.

"Awwwww . . . ," came a chorus of voices, including FuShoe's. One of the braver souls reached out to pet a hairy leg that was as thick as a fence post.

Joey stood before his sensei. He bowed his head and tried to not look at her wickedly taloned bird feet. "I see, Sensei Kendu. It isn't just about knowing how to fight, but when to fight. Thank you for teaching me, Sensei."

Kendu cocked her head down, giving Joey the

unreadable look of a bird. She seemed to have the full range of human emotions, but when she looked at you it was the stare of all raptors—equal parts anger and interest.

Her hand released one rope and grabbed another. She gave a gentle tug. Somewhere in the back of the classroom a hedgehog was falling out of the ceiling at the end of a long bungee. Moments before he had been sleeping; now he was awake and falling. He liked neither of these things. Pulling into the spikiest ball he could, he decided to deliver his most painful greeting to the first thing he encountered.

A moment later the Arachnidarian rattled a gibber of betrayal and outrage. Its glow turned a violent red and chaos spread through the classroom.

As a tentacle pulled Joey away with surprising speed, Sensei Kendu clucked quietly under her breath. She had nothing against either creature or students. This was one of her favorite classes in years. Their solution had impressed her, but this *was* fight class. Standards must be maintained.

Joey woke in the nurse's office. Johnny was there, along with the majority of the class. They were all wrapped in enough bandages to outfit a platoon of mummies. In a room somewhere above them the Arachnidarian was happily purring again. Its clicking gurgle lightly shook the cots, and made the nurse *tsk* with disapproval.

"Oh . . . now I understand," said Joey. "There are some fights you *can't* win."

"Zzayeah," said Johnny. He tried to focus his eyes as he gave a heavily bandaged thumbs-up. "Good class today."

PEONI'S IRRESISTIBLE SECRETS

In which we are given information that
Joey and Johnny would totally pay for.

A few days later Joey and Johnny caught up to Peoni as she hurried across the yard with the box of kittens in her arms. After the dragon attack she had been taking care of them. No one knew where FangSwan had gotten them, and no one was asking. The vice principal said he'd track down good homes.

"Peoni! Where are you running to?" said Joey.

"I'm dropping these kittens off with Zato and then I'm going to dance class!"

"Zato?" questioned Joey. "We never see you anymore, Peoni, and when we do you are always off to see Zato! What is going on?"

Johnny gasped. "Is he teaching you blind swordsman stuff? Can you see colors with your ears?"

"I . . . ," started Peoni. "I don't think Zato can do that, Johnny."

It was hard to tell what their blind vice principal could or could not do. Hearing colors was not out of the question.

"Anyway," continued Peoni, "he's not teaching me blind sword fighting. I'm working on an outside project." She tried to make the last words sound stuffy, and beyond question.

Joey and Johnny had heard this phrase dozens of times all summer and the explanation was not getting any more satisfying. "Peoni! We know it has something to do with the tea party!"

A passing group of Kick Foots gasped as they heard Joey shout this. Tea ceremonies were no laughing matter to ninjas. Statistically, more ninjas have died at tea parties than anywhere else. There was no weapon, monster, or natural disaster more feared. Master Shaggio Footsmear once fought lightning to a standstill, but he still died with a toothpick in his throat.

The topic was taboo. Discussing tea parties at a ninja school was like engaging some snails in a conversation about French restaurants. Most ninjas preferred to forget they had ever existed. Even FangSwan was against them.

MASTER SHAGGIO FOOTSMEAR

Joey pressed forward with his attack. "It IS! You're planning a tea party!" He pointed an accusing finger at her. "You KNOW they're forbidden AND dangerous!" And then he leaned in closer to her ear. "And you *know* we will totally help you. So let us in!"

"Nuh-uh!" said Peoni in a tone that suggested she was three and had a fistful of stolen crayons behind her back. "I . . . uh . . ." She was a terrible liar. Even better, Peoni had not yet picked up on the fact that Joey and Johnny loved to hear her try to lie. It was the only bright spot in her insufferable refusal to tell them her secret.

In a panic, Peoni stared down at the box in her hands. Small paws were pushing through the air holes, taking swipes at her exposed fingers. She had to say something. Something with kittens in it. Maybe she was going to shave them and make cat yarn . . . for a scarf?

"The kittens . . . ," she began, "uh, Zato just needed me to . . ."

"Start a space program for cats," Johnny suggested.

"Look, Igottago! Class!" she sputtered while veering down a staircase that was not in the direction of either of the two places she claimed to be going.

"Well, that was a disappointment!" said Joey, watching her vanish from view. "You should've been patient."

"Yeah, I know," said Johnny. "Last time she said she

was fixing the school's pipe organ, which didn't need fixing . . . *and* we don't actually have one."

"What is going on with that girl?" murmured Joey.

Peoni wandered through the forest surrounding KFA and clattered down a rock staircase she found at the cliff's edge. At the bottom was an old bridge just barely anchored to the mountain by frayed, rotting ropes. If the bridge collapsed, she and the kittens would make a very depressing pile on the rocks that lay a thousand feet below them. Her heartbeat sped up as she approached the halfway point, the bridge creaking and complaining. She held her breath until she got all the way across.

There was a narrow opening in the stone wall to her right that looked like nothing more than a shallow, mossy crack. But when Peoni pushed herself through, it opened into a crude tunnel that led to an equally crude cavern. A lantern was lit for her benefit. Vice Principal Zato was waiting patiently, his arms clasped behind his back and his round black glasses reflecting the flickering light.

"Sorry I'm late, Master Zato," Peoni said as she put the box down.

"Ah," said Zato. He bent down and pulled out a kitten at random. The cat nuzzled the blind man's face before Zato returned it to the box and looked at Peoni in a way that made her brain feel exposed. "How are you doing with the ceremony?"

She ran exasperated fingers through her pointy hair. "There are too many rules! I keep thinking I have them all memorized but then I forget how many pickles are allowed in the sandwiches or—"

Zato interrupted her. "There are *no* pickles allowed in the sandwiches."

"SEE! What would that mistake

get me? An arrow through my head? A flaming ax to my leg?"

"Hmm," Zato considered, "I think the penalty for pickles is death by carnivorous beetle."

"Aaaah!" Peoni's voice slid up and down a scale. "And I'm the only one who can do this?"

"There is no one else."

Peoni waved her finger at the blind man. "You're smart and wise! You have all the rules memorized! Why don't *you* do it?"

"You're very kind, Peoni, but I *do* have my limitations, and I don't just mean my eyes." Zato smiled a little sadly. "I'm sorry, but a ninja tea ceremony must be performed once every thirty years to soothe the spirits of the ninjas it has already claimed."

Zato took in a long, slow breath. He thought of other supernatural catastrophes. Mount Triton, the haunted volcano that buried northern Greece under three feet of glowing green ghostly lava, or the village of Knight's Castle in Maine that slid halfway through the veil to become a literal ghost town. The city's still there, but no one's made it in or out in over fifteen years. Loved ones have to write letters via Oujia boards.

Defeated, Peoni looked around the dank cavern. "Why do we keep meeting in this cave? What's wrong with your office?"

"I've been reminded more than once that it's not *my* office, and mine aren't the only sharp ears in the school."

"FangSwan?"

"He was the sole survivor thirty years ago, and since then has forbidden any mention of it," Zato said. "I would not presume to understand the headmaster's thoughts on the subject. Perhaps you would care to take it up with him."

Peoni shook her head and Zato smiled.

The vice principal produced a cloth sack and placed it next to the box. "Here. You'll need this, but be very careful, it's deli—" He winced slightly as a kitten began to bat at it. Peoni put a hand in to calm them.

"Have you gone to the place I mentioned?" Zato asked as Peoni absently played with the cats.

"No, sir," she said, and then before she could stop herself she blurted, "Why haven't you asked Brad or

Joey and Johnny to do this? They saved the school the last time!"

Zato responded, "They were not the school's only champions, or had you forgotten? The right tool for the right job, Peoni."

"I didn't forget." Peoni smiled. When she raised her head from the box of kittens Zato's round black glasses were staring directly into her eyes.

"Have *you* told Joey and Johnny?"

"No, but they know something's up."

"They are less foolish than they appear . . . possibly." A smile flickered at the corners of Zato's lips. It was there only a moment, but it left him with a new question: "*Why* haven't you told them?"

". . . because YOU told me not to!" Something in the way she paused suggested it was not her only reason.

Zato sighed, trying to hear the words she did not say. He tapped his chin with a finger. "Go to the place I mentioned and talk with the man you find there. He can be . . . difficult, but he can help."

Peoni nodded at the blind man and picked up the cloth sack. As she turned to leave, Zato raised a hand and said in a voice that was not filled with his usual air of certainty, "Perhaps you *should* tell your friends." He couldn't see Peoni's momentary look of anger. "The spirits grow more restless every day and I fear what will happen if they don't resume their slumber. Before this is all over, we may need some things head-butted or hit with a hammer."

"*I* can hit things with a hammer!" Peoni declared with enough force to snuff out Zato's unneeded lantern.

"Then we shall have to get you a hammer," Zato said, amused. "Ask Johnny, maybe you can borrow his."

She walked out of the cavern, leaving the vice principal in darkness. Now she was late for dance class and she'd have to lie about why.

8

KNOW YOUR ENEMY

In which Sensei Renbow's day
is completely ruined.

The whip-crack sound pulled the class momentarily out of its stupor, but as soon as the students realized it was just Sensei Renbow being too hard on the chalk they settled right back into it again. Their professor was ferociously writing names on a series of boards and hurriedly circling, crossing out, and drawing cartoon blood droplets over some of the names as he spoke.

". . . and *that's* when Migosh"—he circled the name in red with his usual exaggerated flourish—"killed Tengue"—a red X was slashed through this name on another chalkboard—"who was his best friend until he discovered his secret affair with the beautiful yet

treacherous Kreshalla!" Over this last name, Renbow
drew hearts and daggers.

Things were getting desperate in the room. The
class had been going on for four hours and it most likely
wouldn't end until someone managed to figure out
what Sensei Renbow was trying to illustrate for them.

"You can't make an omelet without breaking some

eggs?" squeaked a weak voice from the back of the room.

"No, no, no!" Renbow dismissively waved his hand. "You are missing the point completely! Let's go back over the part where Yosh MeSook falls in love with the Demon Babhast, who has just kidnapped the village barber's daughter, Lifonia, and plans to exchange souls with her!" He spun around to face his class wearing a fanged mask with blazing blue eyes and horns. "THIS is the face of Babhast the jealous demon! What does that tell you?"

Johnny raised his hand and answered, "That you *can* always judge a book by its cover?"

"What?!" said Renbow, pulling the mask down and frowning at his student. "No! That's not what it should . . ."

"Bad guys got fangs!" another student called out.

"No! NO! That's not even a saying! Remember back when I told you the part about how King Groman won his fortune but then died before he could spend a penny . . ."

Joey raised a hand and shouted, "A penny saved should be spent immediately!"

"That is not even how that goes, and that's not what I was—"

"Isn't 'spend a penny' a British way of saying you gotta go to the bathroom?"

Renbow turned to Spratt. "What does that have to do with what we were just discussing, Spratt?"

"Nothing, sir," said Spratt, "I just have to spend a penny!"

"A fool and his money are soon parted!" shouted Johnny.

"Hey!" Spratt said. "I've been keeping this money in the bank since the beginning of class!"

"Careful, guys, his cup runneth over!"

"Stop it! STOP IT!" Renbow threw his hands out as if he was shielding himself from an arrow attack. "You!" Renbow said, pointing at Spratt. "Go . . . do what you need to do." Spratt wasted no time in running out of the room. "The rest of you: focus on the lesson."

"If you see a penny, don't pick it up!"

"Grrraah," choked Renbow, his mustache bristling. "No, Joey, that is not how it goes." The teacher turned back to the snarl of scribbled names on his chalkboards, whispering to himself in an attempt to regain his place in the story. "Did I already cover Rignaldo being betrayed by six of his sons while he himself betrayed the seventh son who was the only one who remained true to his father?" There was a slight hum in the room as every student said "ummmm" in unison.

"What about Handsome Hendo professing his love to the ravishing Shalta, who had secretly plotted his death but instead was poisoned by Baltho, Hendo's best friend, who discovered Shalta's plot, and then he himself was murdered by the grief-stricken Hendo?"

There was the sharp sound of a hand slapping a desk followed by an exuberant, "Oh, sir! I've seen this."

Renbow turned to see Johnny's hand waving frantically for his attention. Instinctively the professor put a hand to his forehead. "No, Johnny, you couldn't have seen this—"

"I saw it with my grandmother."

"Oh?" said Renbow, hope timidly peeking from his heart. "Your grandmother took you to see the epic of *Kosh Kiosh*?"

"It sure sounds like it."

Renbow trembled with excitement. "Did she perhaps take you to see the production directed by Sir Frederick Gransacko? He performed it only three times."

"No," said Johnny, furrowing his brow in concentration, "I'm pretty sure it was sponsored by Benson's Overnight Denture Bucket."

"What? No."

"Yeah!" Johnny continued, taking no notice of his teacher's horrified expression. "And it wasn't called what you called it. It's called *Days of Hearts Bleeding*. It's still her favorite two hours of the day!"

Renbow clutched at one of his chalkboards to keep from falling over. "You . . . you're talking about a . . . a soap . . . a soap opera!" he finished with a gasp.

"I don't remember soap, sir, just dentures and boredom."

"No, Johnny. No! This"—he waved his arm at the boards around him—"this is the highest art. It's the most epic, sweeping story ever told! It takes three full weeks just to perform the first act. A good director expects that some of the audience members will die just trying to watch the whole thing." He banged on the table, sending a cloud of chalk dust into the air. "There is nothing better!"

"Well, yeah, that's exactly what my granny said."

Renbow sank to the floor, clutching his head. "They turned *Kosh Kiosh* into a soap opera!"

"Fool me once, shame on me! Fool me twice, uh . . ."

"Go! Fs for all of you. Class dismissed!" said Renbow in a choked voice.

"What?" said Joey. "We failed?"

"The whole world has failed. Since you are in the world, then you have failed too! Art is dead!" Renbow sat on the floor, feebly waving an arm toward the door.

The Kick Foots gathered up their belongings and silently fled the room. Joey nearly made it all the way out, but an irresistible force pulled at him, making him spin on his heels and walk back into the classroom. Johnny tried to snag him by the arm.

"No!" Johnny whispered at him from the safety

of the corridor. "Don't! If the lion fails to bore you to death you shouldn't get him talking . . . or words to that effect!"

"Sir?" said Joey to his professor, who sat on the floor stroking the leather spines of his thirty-eight-volume set of the epic of *Kosh Kiosh*. "What was the saying for today? I really need to know."

Sensei Renbow hugged one of his beloved books and looked at Joey with sad, wet eyes. "Know your enemy," he croaked, "because your enemy might not have fangs and horns and bulging red eyes. Know your enemy!"

9

FANGS AND HORNS AND BULGING RED EYES

In which a matter of Tims
is discussed.

The man with the circular saw for a right hand was scratching his chin. This was a terrible idea. As is replacing your hand with a circular saw. Anyway, the man found a hair there. Just a single harmless hair, but it stood out obnoxiously on his otherwise perfectly smooth chin. The scratching had just started to feel good when the saw roared to life.

"YAA!" he said, pulling the saw away from his face milliseconds before his chin was added to the clutter on his desk.

Scar EyeFace turned to the small, glowing lens and spoke into it: "Io, get the maintenance guy up here to check on my arm, I nearly cut my head off!"

"Very good, sir," replied a pleasant mechanical voice from a speaker in the desk. "I will send in Tim."

"Oh, and this hair on my chin needs to be dealt with!"

"Immediately, I will send in Tim."

He opened his mouth to question the last statement when there was a knock on the door. It opened remotely after the jab of one of the many buttons under the desk. A man walked across the spacious office and made himself more at home than Scar Eye-Face would've liked.

"Howdy, skipper! I'm Tim from maintenance!" Tim wore a drab and dingy jumpsuit. His every motion was unbearably perky.

The office was designed to be imposing. People were supposed to feel uncomfortable. Its looming curved wall of windows had been tinted to make the outside world always look overcast and slightly distorted. The only chair for guests was against the far wall. If you wanted to sit you had to walk over, pick up the chair (which was unnecessarily heavy), and drag it in front of the desk. At meeting's end you'd have to decide whether to lug it back or awkwardly leave it there. Still, the room seemed unable to sour Tim's chipper mood.

EyeFace could feel his ire building.

The saw sprang to life again, forcing him to jerk with surprise. "This keeps happening!" he said, thrusting the still-spinning blade toward the maintenance man.

"Oh yeah!" said the man. "That'll happen."

"I want that *not* to happen!" growled Scar EyeFace as the blade spun faster.

Tim pulled out a small folding computer from his work belt. He plugged it into the terrifying arm and starting tapping away on the keyboard. A few *bleeps* and *bloops* later, the saw powered down. Tim nodded his head in a knowing fashion.

"Weeeell, sir, what ya got here is a spinning blade of destruction hooked directly up to yer anger centers."

"My anger centers?" EyeFace said. "Why is it hooked up to my . . . Wait, is *that* why it was running all day yesterday? That's why I don't have my beautiful ceramic giraffes anymore?" Just the memory of it overrode whatever Tim had done. The saw began to turn.

Tim took notice of the sad remains of delicate ceramic legs scattered about the room. "It's cybernetic. Gotta be hooked up to some part of yer brain, sir! Figger something musta got jostled last time you were in fer . . ."

"*Figger* out something else!" shouted Scar EyeFace, the whirring blade spinning faster than ever.

A few more *boops* and the angry saw went offline again. There were a few moments of silence before there was another knock at the door.

"Hello, sir, I'm Tim, your barber," said a man in a tight white shirt and an elaborate mustache.

"You're a Tim, too?" Scar EyeFace asked, careful to keep his saw limb away from anything essential.

"I can explain that, sir," interrupted Tim from maintenance. "Io had a small hiccup a couple of months ago, began firing anyone on your staff not named Tim."

"You mean I have nothing but Tims working for me?"

Maintenance Tim sucked air through his teeth.

"Weeeeell, mostly, yeah, but me and the Tims fixed it; she hired a couple of Freds just last week!"

"A *couple* of Freds?"

"Aw nuts!" Tim from maintenance pulled a notepad from his pocket and jotted something down. "I better make sure she's not just hiring Freds."

"Tim," said Scar EyeFace, "take care of this hair on my chin."

"I should really keep working on the arm, sir."

"BARBER Tim!"

"Ah, right, that should have been obvious."

Barber Tim pulled a pair of thick glasses down from his forehead and peered closely at the offending hair. With a pair of tweezers, he yanked it out by the root. The yelp that EyeFace emitted was accompanied by a sudden roar of the saw.

"Tim, why did that happen?" he asked in alarm.

Barber Tim opened his mouth.

"Maintenance Tim!" shouted Scar EyeFace. "But . . . as long as you're here I could use a trim."

Barber Tim closed his mouth and got to work. Maintenance Tim answered, "I hooked the saw up to your pain centers. It won't whirr when yer mad no more!"

"I'm trying to remain calm, I really am, Tim. But the last twenty-four hours have been a trial. Let me get this straight . . . now, my saw will turn on if I stub my toe?"

Maintenance Tim looked back down at his keyboard. "I see your point." He rapidly started typing again, the circular saw periodically going on and off.

Scar EyeFace took a deep breath and turned toward his desk. "Io, take some notes."

"Very well, sir."

He settled back into his leather chair while the two Tims went about their business. "Pirate Captain Cornelius Loon contacted me. He has agreed to wreck the ninja tea ceremony. In exchange I promised him the location of the Great Tooth."

"Excellent, sir!" A red light on the transmitter dimmed and brightened, the only way Io could nod. "And you know where that is?"

"I do." He smiled. "More or less. I told them to start at Kick Foot Academy. Of course, they'll need to find a way in without alerting FangSwan. If they do alert him we'll need to immediately find a replacement crew of pirates."

"I will compile a list of candidates for you, sir."

"Really? Hmm. Also, Cornelius is uncommonly clever—for a pirate. It's in their nature to double-cross.

We should come up with . . . we should . . ."

Scar EyeFace had grown so used to his saw randomly turning on and off as Maintenance Tim tried connecting it to different parts of his brain that the prolonged stillness broke his concentration. Tim had stopped working and seemed to be lost in thought.

"What is it now?"

"Just evening out the back, sir."

"MAINTENANCE TIM!"

Barber Tim pouted. Maintenance Tim was caught a bit off guard. He was slightly less chipper when he asked, "Why . . . why wouldja attach a circular saw to yer hand, anyway?"

"It was my grandfather's," EyeFace said flatly. It was not the answer either Tim had expected. There were no follow-up questions.

"What was I saying, Io?"

Io was quick to respond. "Cornelius Loon. Smart pirate. Possible double cross. Perhaps we should . . . give him more incentive?"

Scar EyeFace's bulging left eye glinted with glee. "Make sure his crew thinks there's treasure under that teahouse. That ought to keep them interested."

"And what about your ninjas, sir? Joey and Johnny?"

"What about them?"

"I do not see a profit margin in disrupting the tea ceremony."

"There's always cash to be made from chaos," Eye-Face said. "Anyway, this isn't about that. Those two made it personal after the Red Moon fiasco."

WISEMAN NOTE: Not true. Scar EyeFace remained so deep in the shadows during that "fiasco" that the boys didn't even know who he was.

"In fact, I want Joey to—" The saw turned on again, cutting off his thoughts but thankfully nothing else. Scar EyeFace looked at it and said, "Johnny." The saw spun faster.

"I can change it, sir," said Maintenance Tim, looking up from his keyboard.

"No!" Scar EyeFace smiled. "I think you got it right this time, Tim."

"Thank you, sir," both Tims said, and for once their boss was so happy he didn't bother to correct them.

PEONI CLIMBS A MOUNTAIN

In which Peoni . . . uh, climbs a . . . mountain?

The mountain that Peoni had been directed to looked taller and sharper than any she'd seen. It loomed above the others around it like an enormous stone dagger stabbing the clouds.

The air rang with foreboding—literally. From somewhere high above the clouds the spectral sound of chanting haunted the air:

"Foreboding . . . foreboding . . . foreboding . . ."

WISEMAN NOTE: This is less frightening than you might think. The Lovers of the Lovely Word are a small band of monks who honor the gift of language by choosing a single word and chanting it for a month. If Peoni had shown up two weeks earlier, the mountainside would've rung with the sound of "skedaddle."

"You can both come out now," Peoni grumbled. Spinning on her heel, she faced the only two shrubs on the otherwise flat clearing. She hadn't seen them move, but they had clearly not been there before.

"Hi, Peoni," Johnny said, standing up from behind his foliage camouflage. Then both he and Peoni turned toward the second bush.

"I don't know about that other guy, but I'm just a hedge," Joey said.

Peoni rolled her eyes. "Zato put me on a secret mission. What part of 'secret mission' is so hard to understand? Why can't you guys leave me alone?"

"Because we want to help." Joey had not stood up yet. His words shook the bush as he spoke.

"I agree with the hedge," said Johnny. "Anyway, we already know your secret."

"We're here. We're helping. Why can't you accept that?"

"Because . . . augh! I am not debating this with a

stupid shrub." Peoni stomped over, grabbed Joey's hedge, and threw it into the trees. Joey looked indignant and dusted himself off.

Peoni continued. "I can't accept it because you know it's a secret mission, but you yell 'tea ceremony!' in a crowded hallway. Because you think the solution to every problem is to punch it into submission."

"No, we don't," Joey said, frantically trying to think of a single example to support his statement.

"We didn't punch *you* into submission," said Johnny. Although it could be argued that that is exactly what they were doing. They just weren't using their fists.

"You know I'm the best stealth student KFA has ever seen," Peoni said.

It was true, Peoni was currently in the most advanced stealth class KFA offered, which taught a technique created by Master Anonymous Anybody. It was a sort of low-impact martial art—*very* low. You weren't even supposed to make eye contact. Like many disciplines, there was a belt system to indicate levels of expertise. From lowest level to highest, the stealth system went: neon, Day-Glo, apparent, plain, camouflage, translucent, clear, ghost, obscured, invisible, and whatwhere?

WISEMAN NOTE: The greatest experts in this technique meet once a year to compete in the world's most grueling game of hide-and-seek.

Supposedly there can only be one Master of the Unseen at any time, but really . . . how would they know?

"So?" Joey asked.

"So . . ." Peoni pointed at Joey. "There's no way you can follow me if I don't want you to!"

Joey pushed his forehead into Peoni's outstretched finger. "We *know* you're heading to the top of the mountain. We don't *have* to follow you!"

The two ninjas stared at each other. Johnny looked nervously back and forth between them.

"That's . . . a valid point," Peoni said.

Mountain climbing is very hard and deadly dangerous. Mountains tend to be very steep. Also, they are made out of rocks and trees and other not-soft things. Plus they're rather cold at the top. They are the exact reason why elevators were invented. To scale a mountain requires the right equipment, supplies, a plan, and occasionally sherpas. Joey, Johnny, and Peoni had none of those things. Instead they had a few years of ninja training and a begrudging truce to work together. At least until they got to the summit.

The higher they went the harder it got. They moved doggedly, slowly pushing upward. Securing one handhold, then another, and another. Occasionally a pebble would pull free from the mountain and fall past them with increasing speed, demonstrating exactly what they hoped would not happen to them. It was a relief when they reached the cloud layer and could no longer see the ground. It was still there, of course, but they didn't need to be constantly reminded every time they looked down. What the young ninjas lacked in mountaineering skills they made up in improvisation. Joey let the others stand on his shoulders, then belly flopped across a small ravine like a human bridge. Peoni threw a series of shurikens into the sheer rock face for them to use as toeholds, while Johnny pounded ledges into the mountain with his hammer, which today he had dubbed "Mr. Mallory."

"Whatever's at the top of this mountain better be awesome!" Johnny declared.

Peoni hung a foot down so Joey could swing across a small gap. "Are you kidding?" Joey said, establishing a solid toehold. "Look at how hard this is! Whatever's at the top is going to be epic."

Johnny gritted his teeth as the wind knocked his dooley-bopper against the mountain and back into his face. A couple of small stones broke free and joined an ever-growing number far below.

"So stuff is worth more if it's hard to get to?" Johnny asked.

"Yes . . . ?" Joey unfastened his sash and threw one end to Peoni. She grabbed it and Joey slingshotted her higher up the mountain. Then she hooked her toes under an exposed scrub root, flipped upside down, and helped the boys up in a similar fashion.

"So if I had a penny, but it was on the moon, how much is that worth?"

"A buck seventy-five," said Joey.

"Cool."

At times, Peoni wondered whether the boys' constant blather was taking her mind off the grueling

climb or driving her crazy. The question would have to wait until they reached the top. If she pushed either of them over the edge, she'd have her answer.

It was nearing sunset when Peoni's hand appeared at the lip of another seemingly endless series of ledges. Pulling herself up, she smiled and turned to drag Joey up after her.

"If this isn't the top, I'm going home," he said. It was

and he didn't. Six hours had elapsed since the beginning of their ascent. Bodies bruised, muscles strained, and fingernails chipped, Joey, Johnny, and Peoni had arrived at the summit.

WISEMAN NOTE: Some of you might scoff at that number and declare that no one could scale a real mountain in six hours. Some of you are not ninjas.

THE WISEMAN WHO IS WONDERFUL AND WISE

In which you, the lazy reader, are gifted with wisdom you didn't earn.

The top of the mountain was a roughly circular landing with an uneven rocky surface and the occasional patch of pale green lichen. To the west the ground rose to a slightly higher peak, about ten feet tall. At the top was a slender man, seated in the lotus position and silhouetted by the rays of the setting sun. His beard gently rustled in the wind; his body seemed completely immune to the crisp mountain air.

"Greetings, seekers of knowledge. You have traveled far. How may my wisdom be of service?" It was a rich voice, filled with intrigue. There was an understandable moment of awed silence as the three ninjas marveled, watching beams of light spread out in an almost angelic fashion.

"Normally, now you ask a question and then tip generously," the voice prompted.

"Hi, sir," said Joey and Johnny in unison.

"Oh, great. It's you two."

The enigmatic figure on the summit's summit? That was me. I'm a wiseman. THE wiseman for Lemming Falls and the lands surrounding. The job description requires me to be a font of wisdom and knowledge, and I'm one of the best, if I do say so myself. Wisemanery requires a ton of experience, an excellent education, a knack for improvisation, and a solid internet connection. Trust me, no one wants to climb a mountain just to hear you say, "Your guess is as good as mine."

On top of the standard "Where is love?" questions (more common than you might think), I also have to be up-to-date on all of the weird stuff that pertains to my specific location, including superheroes, giant robots, alternate dimensions, and (sigh) . . . Joey and Johnny, the ninjas.

"Good to see you, too, sir," Johnny said.

"Wait! You guys know each other?" Peoni asked, then threw up her hands in frustration. "Of COURSE you know each other!"

The last time I saw them we were on the astral plane.

They mistook me for the Grim Reaper, and, in a state of terror, beat me up. Ahhh, good times.

"So . . . ," I said, allowing my voice to go flat. "This qualifies as an official visit. Give me your questions."

Joey and Peoni rested their hands on their chins in thought. Johnny raised his like an overzealous schoolboy. "Oh, here's one! Why do you live at the top of a mountain?"

I smiled and put on my best mystic face. "Perhaps I live on the top of every mountain—"

"Oooh. Deep!" Johnny said.

"—perhaps I own a helicopter."

The effort to understand made Johnny's dooleybopper bounce with delight. After a moment he cleared his mind with characteristic ease. "Okay! Next question—"

"No."

"Amazing! I haven't even asked my question yet," Johnny gasped.

I bowed my head to him and smiled. It might help soften the blow. "You misunderstand. Only one question per pilgrim per visit. Want another question? Then you will have to return to the bottom of the mountain and climb back up."

That made all of their eyes widen. The sun sank a little lower. Johnny raised a hand and asked, "Why?"

"I'm sorry, I cannot answer that question."

Eight hours later a shaking hand rose above the lip of the summit. It was followed by another, and then Johnny's masked face, dripping with sweat. He pulled himself up and sprawled, panting, on the ground. Say what you want, the boy made good time.

Joey and Peoni quickly finished the hot dogs they'd been eating and rushed to his side. "Johnny, you okay?" Joey asked, his words slightly muffled by hot dog crumbs.

With Peoni's help, Johnny eased into a sitting position and slowly reined in his gasping breaths. He rose to his feet and climbed the low hill until we were eye to eye. When he spoke, his voice rang out with eight hours of determination.

"Why?"

"That is the way it has always been."

"Really?"

"I'm sorry, I cannot answer that question."

Johnny stomped angrily to the edge of the mountaintop. He pushed up his sleeves and braced himself for the climb down, "Okay, you wait there, old man." His voice was firm. "I'll be back in eight hours! Gravity will not defeat my thirst for knowledge."

Johnny began to lower himself down, but Joey stopped him. Peoni remained rooted to the spot, rubbing her forehead. Joey gently tugged at Johnny's arm. "Johnny, why are you doing this?"

"Because he is an idiot," I said from behind.

"NanaNaNoNOnoNO!" Joey spun around, panic in his voice. "That was not my question!"

Peoni grabbed Johnny by the dooley-bopper and pulled the boys over into a huddle. "Johnny, you stay. We can do this."

Between Johnny's first and second questions, Peoni and Joey had worked out a rough agreement on how the boys would be allowed to help. The negotiations were long and labored, but they had plenty of time.

"Technically this is still Peoni's mission," Joey said, "so we need to follow her lead."

"*Technically?*" growled Peoni. "At best you are my flunkies, got it?"

"How about 'minions'?" Johnny said. "Sounds way cooler."

"Fine," said Peoni, already fearing that this mission was starting to spiral out of her control.

Peoni explained what she knew. There are tens of thousands—no, hundreds of thousands—of specific rules of conduct at a proper ninja tea party. Each rule broken is another potential death waiting to happen. Just defending yourself from your first broken rule will very likely cause you to break more rules. It doesn't matter how good a ninja you are, the math will get you in the end. Which is something every grade-schooler already knows in his bones.

To be fair, many of rules are linked to specific seasons, so if you know what season the party will be held in, you can cut that number down to fifty or sixty thousand rules (more for a winter tea party—there're presents and a specific way to shovel the walk).

"So there," she said proudly, "I've already eliminated like eighty-nine thousand ways to die."

"No," Joey told her, "you knew it was in the spring. There's a difference."

Peoni glowered and folded her arms. "It's my mission. I don't need your help. I'm just allowing you to because you'd bug me until I let you."

"That's probably true." Joey gave her a smile, but did not get one in return.

"Why do we need to have a tea party at all?" asked Johnny. "I thought FangSwan banned them."

"It's because—because . . ." Peoni pondered an amazing lie involving a time-traveling ferret, but in the end simply said, "Because Zato said so. It has something to do with the restless spirits."

"Restless spirits? They're the worst kind," Johnny said. "Remember, spirits equals ghosts equals dead guys equals zombies. And I *hate* zombies! They're surprisingly resistant to clown hammers."

"And Zato's enough reason for me. He kept Fang-Swan from killing us, like, six times since summer started," Joey said.

The boys listened as Peoni went over everything that needed to be done. The ceremony had to be perfect. That included memorization of all the rules (it's not that they *would* be called on *all* of them, but they *could* be called on *any* of them). It also meant performing them with grace and precision. A spilled drop on the tablecloth could earn you a face full of bees, or worse.

Then there was the tea itself. Most ceremonies allowed the host to choose the tea to be served, and woe to the guest whose palate couldn't distinguish oolong from Earl Grey. But these were spirits and they required a very specific kind of tea. The only tea they could drink. A perfect cup of tea . . . that no one seemed to know how to brew.

While they planned I replenished the oil in the lanterns that lit the summit. It had been dark since before Johnny got back, and it's hard enough to see ninjas in the daylight. I didn't want them to sneak up on me and ruin my mystic mojo. Finally, Joey returned with his question.

"You ready?" I asked him. "Don't mess it up. You only got one."

Joey closed his eyes and whispered the question to himself five different ways. Once he found one he liked, he took a deep breath and said, "How do I make spirit tea?"

People think wisemen know everything. We don't. At least not all at once. My mind is like a vast library, but imagine every book, article, and picture connected by colored strings of experience. Many items have more than one string, forming a grand web of knowledge and abstract thought. It's this disorganization that allows me to make the leaps of intuition that keep the pilgrims climbing that mountain.

We all have our tricks for stalling when we need time to think. Nubble Plum the Patient had this wonderful knack for sleeping while sitting. This allowed him to take a catnap after being asked a question, and it just made him look thoughtful. Personally I couldn't do that, due to the snoring. Ruins the illusion.

So, I fluffed up my beard and pretended my arms were snakes. Slowly wiggling them back and forth. My eyes rolled in their sockets up toward the moon. I knew the answer already, I just needed a little time to work on my poetry. Then I waited some more, until Joey looked suitably impressed.

"To brew a tea spirits deem perfect
These four objects you must first collect:
Fire from wood with uncommon trait
Tea in the shadow of heroes great
Water is gathered high in the blue
The teapot, of course, right behind you."

Both Joey and Johnny spun to look behind them.
"Not literally," groaned Peoni.

Joey was undeterred. "Still . . . did you hear that!
THAT is why you come to see a wiseman!"

Sometimes I forget that the boys aren't all bad. The
way Joey was pointing at me and smiling—it made me
blush.

"Pure mystic mumbo jumbo, right from the source. Not a clue what it means, but when it happens, we'll be all, 'OoooOOoooh.'" Joey waved his hands in a poor imitation of me.

"Thanks." I was understandably grumpy as the pretty girl ninja with the spiky hair approached. But when Peoni performed a pleasant curtsey aimed at showing respect, it did warm my heart a little.

So when she asked, "How can I make sure the tea ceremony works, sir?" I whispered the answer in her ear as plainly as I could, but it didn't seem to make her happy. She slumped back toward her fellow ninjas.

"What'd he say? What'd he say?" asked Johnny. "Is the answer 'pudding'?"

"No," she said. "Why would you think it's pudding?"

"I want pudding," Johnny admitted.

"Well, don't hold back! Tell us," Joey urged.

Peoni looked from Joey to Johnny and back again. A private smile curled her lip. "He told me that both of you have to take dancing lessons from Sensei Woo."

"No he didn't!" Joey said. He turned to me and shouted, "No you didn't. Did you?"

"I'm sorry, I cannot answer that question."

"Really?"

"Or that one."

"Monkeynuggets," Johnny said. "Do we have to wear tutus?"

Soon they were getting ready to go. Peoni's mood soured slightly as she pondered the answer to her question. Conversely, Joey was exploding with joy as he ran through different possible answers to the tea riddle. A mumbling stream of consciousness occasionally burbled out of his mouth. Johnny was off exploring the perimeter of the summit. After a time he came running back.

"Guys, I— The wiseman's gone! He's flying away in a helicopter."

Slightly annoyed at the interruption, Joey said, "Johnny, I think the helicopter was only a metaphor."

Johnny stopped and double-checked the sky. A small whirling machine gently disappeared into the predawn mountain air. "Okay. The wiseman is flying away in a metaphor."

"What's next?" asked Peoni.

Joey said, "We'll go figure out the tea and you work on the rest! That's fair, right? We'll run the errands while you do the important stuff." Peoni looked less than enthused, despite the boys' double thumbs-up. Joey turned to Johnny. "Johnny, let's start in Lemming

Falls. There's lots of heroes there, and it's basically in KFA's backyard. That's kinda behind us, right? That's two parts of the riddle right there."

"Cool," Johnny said. "And we can see Knight-Lite! I say we go right after we find something to eat."

"Why don't you get a hot dog?" Peoni told him.

"What hot d—" was as far as Johnny got. Suddenly, there before him appeared Mack's Enlightened Hots and Grub. The years of serving this particular venue had rubbed off on Mack, and now, like all forms of higher thinking, his food cart presented itself only to those who actively sought it out.

"Getcha hot dogs!" Mack hollered in a matter-of-fact manner. "Hot dogs! Getcha enlightened hot dogs. Can't ponder the mysteries of the universe on an empty stomach."

The ninjas approached the cart and bought some fuel for the trip down. Mack jumped on their orders, his thick arms working quickly, flipping burgers, drenching fries with cheese and chili, and slopping sauerkraut on the hots.

"Why dontcha grab a coupla sodas, kids. Contemplating the universe's inner workings can be thirsty work," said Mack.

"Wow," Johnny said, "kind of a rough location."

"Yeah, it's a bear. What'll ya have? Hot Dog of Enlightenment? All-Knowing Burger?"

Johnny pointed to one of the patties on the grill. "Can you make me one with everything?"

Mack snickered. "That's funny, kid." But Johnny was too busy slurping up his soda to notice.

KNIGHT-LITE
WINKS A LOT

In which old friends are reunited
and given the bird.

"**G**uys!" Knight-Lite cheered and ran to hug the both of them. Or at least he would have if he hadn't tripped over nothing and gone rolling across the floor. Flat on his back, the sidekick said, "Golly, it's so good to see you!"

Johnny gave him a hand up. "Any chance you'll be coming back to KFA?"

"I hope to next year," Knight-Lite chirped. "Night-Knight wanted me to focus on death traps. Specifically, escaping them."

"Oooh, I bet Professor McJones could build an amazing death trap," Johnny said.

"He *is* a death trap." Joey shuddered, haunted by the ghosts of a thousand Band-Aids.

They were walking through the wide entrance hall of an enormous gothic mansion, a darkened corridor that seemed to stretch on forever. The only light came from glass display cases positioned at regular intervals. Inside they featured suit after suit of medieval armor, like some giant's toy army, *mint in box*.

"It's like we're at a Knight-Lite family reunion," Joey whispered to Johnny. Knight-Lite, sidekick to Night-Knight, was dressed in spandex and steel, a costume that fit into the world of superheroes while remaining true to the medieval theme that was the duo's trademark. Between its red-plumed helmet, micro-Kevlar weave, and self-deploying shield, Knight-Light's costume was one of the safest in the superhero world. Which was good, because he really needed it.

The hapless sidekick spent most of his time getting captured by various villains only to be saved at the last minute. Word on the street was that Night-Knight took on a squire only because he was defeating his rogues' gallery too easily and needed an Achilles' heel. This was unfair, as Knight-Lite was a technical whiz, helping to repair or improve most of the tools and weaponry in Night-Knight's armory. Obsessed with superheroes, he was also a nearly limitless database for superhero trivia. His only problem lay with the actual superhero-ing itself.

"So why are we here again?" asked Johnny.

"This is the stately manor of Sir Edmund Dusk," Knight-Lite said. "He's *really good friends* with Night-Knight. If fact, you could *almost* say they were like *brothers.*"

"Do you have something in your eye? Why are you winking so much?" Joey asked.

Knight-Lite opened his mouth to speak, made several starts, but no real words came out.

"So why are we here again?" asked Johnny.

"Oh? Oh yeah. Peoni told me all about Ting. I think *Night-Knight and Sir Dusk* might be able to help."

"There it is again with the winking," Joey said. "Are you okay?"

As Lemming Falls's wealthiest man, Sir Edmund Dusk had set up a wide variety of charities to help the city, many of them associated with the exploits of Night-Knight, the world's most medieval detective. One of these, the Committee for a Lovely Lemming, focuses on cleaning up after superhero scuffles. Currently it was helping to repair the damage done to the civic center when Emperor Worm attempted to smash Night-Knight with the world's second-largest fly swatter.

The Common Sense Squad visits various villains in jail, trying to convince them to use their powers to help society. For example, the Float Master robbed three convenience stores for a total of $704.96 before being captured. Instead he could've been making a legal fortune with his technology. When he sold the rights to his antigravity ray to help cover his court costs, that yielded seven-point-two million dollars. He was literally on the ceiling with joy, but that had more to do with his ray having backfired while he was fighting

Night-Knight. The Float Master is, now and forever, falling up. When he goes outside you have to tie a string around him like a big balloon.

The charity Knight-Lite specifically brought Joey and Johnny here to see was Capes and Critters. It was formed to take care of and rehabilitate the pets of supervillains after they'd gone to jail. Finding homes for various puppies, cats, and box turtles was simple enough, but C&C also took care of the more difficult cases.

The Mako Master had a shiver of sharks at his beck and call. After his crime wave was broken on the shores of justice, they certainly couldn't just be released to the wild. Not after he had taught them how to rob banks. Doctor DoEvil had an African gray parrot that could tear you apart. Not with beak and claw, but with biting sarcasm and devastating assaults on your self-worth. Even worse, it just rolled its eyes any time you talked to it.

WISEMAN NOTE: That parrot was so cruel that Night-Knight only managed to defeat the bird with the help of Deaf-Devil, the man who couldn't hear fear.

Then there were the special cases. Skeletal horses, fire-breathing death monkeys, and radioactive spiders. They had an amoeba the size of a school bus. An entire wing was dedicated to Mix 'n' Match's menagerie. He was a brilliant geneticist/zookeeper and had used his twisted intellect to create chimeras, including the deadly rhinomoose, the less-deadly moosemongoose, and even a moosemouse. Mix 'n' Match kinda had a thing about moose.

The goal was to eventually find homes for the animals, but not just anybody can adopt a nuclear-powered llama. It was pretty slow going.

The Dusk Estates were on the far edge of the city. There was plenty of room to house the beasts in a series of buildings behind the main mansion. Teams of experts were called in to see to their well-being, keeping the animals safe as well as protecting the general public. Despite all their unusual abilities and powers, only the curious catbird routinely escaped from its enclosure. Though that was hardly a problem. Once outside it would stalk, chase, and finally catch itself.

"This is BrainBeak," Knight-Lite said at the end of the tour.

"That is completely terrifying," Joey said. On the other side of the glass was a black-and-red hawk about the size of a large eagle. A viciously curved beak opened wide and a snakelike tongue tasted the air as they approached. On her breast there was a pattern of feathers that looked like a blood-red lightning bolt.

"All raptors look a little scary," Knight-Lite said. "It's the brow." Beneath that brow her eyes were a milky white with an ice-gray iris. Even when she wasn't looking at you, she seemed to see you.

Johnny bobbed his head left and right, a movement only exaggerated by his dooley-bopper. "Look, I'm making her dance," Johnny said. Indeed, the bird was bouncing up and down on her perch, matching Johnny's movements.

"I've heard nothing but good things about Brain-Beak's rehabilitation. When she first came here she used to go right for the eyes, but now she's a good bird.

Aren't you a good bird, Brainy?" In answer she opened her beak and made a sound so shrill and savage all of Joey's arm hair spontaneously tried to escape through his sleeve.

"Why, you must be Joey and Johnny," a friendly voice boomed out behind them. "I'm Edmund Dusk."

"Pleasure to meet you, sir," the boys said.

"Call me Eddie."

Eddie was tall, handsome, and broad-shouldered. His square jaw held an easy smile and his voice carried an upper-crust British accent. Joey noted that, despite his large frame, Sir Dusk had also managed to sneak up on them, which wasn't an easy thing to do to a ninja. Of course, the bird might've helped.

"My ward has told me all about you." He smiled. "Wonderful to finally meet you both."

"What 'word'?" Johnny asked.

Dusk blinked and coughed into his hand. "Uh, I mean young Knight-Lite here. Told me all about you."

Once again Knight-Lite was furiously winking at the boys.

Sir Dusk carried on: "Until Night-Knight put her away, BrainBeak was a creature of the dreaded Mr. Mindstorm. Poor bird was born blind and Mindstorm raised her inside a chamber that he bombarded with his psychorays. Over time they changed her, allowed her to see through the eyes of others, and more."

"So can she read your mind?" Joey said. He quickly eyed the fiendish-looking fowl, wondering if she could see inside his head. Did she know just how much he didn't like bird feet?

"Oh, no," laughed Dusk. "At least I don't think so. BrainBeak doesn't seem to be any smarter than others of her kind, but she can lock onto a person's brain waves and find them anywhere in the world . . . theoretically."

"We could use her to send a letter to Ting!" Johnny said. "Good thinking, Knight-Lite."

"Yes, jolly good," said Sir Dusk. Knight-Lite blushed with pleasure.

They spent a few moments with BrainBeak, learning how to communicate with her. Sir Dusk showed them the proper way to tie a message onto her leg, and gave them two falconer's gloves. The dull brown leather gloves were made from triple-thick buffalo hide and reinforced with steel on the inside. Eddie warned them that BrainBeak's talons could crush their wrist bones into powder without them. The knowledge made Joey's legs feel hollow and filled with spiders.

So it was a great relief to Joey when they attached a letter and sent the horrid bird on her first delivery.

"Ting's going to be so surprised," Johnny said.

"Yes . . . ," Joey agreed. "He is."

Hi Ting,

Great news! Brad's alive and he saved himself! You can come home now!

Sorry it took so long, but we had to figure out how to reach you. Meet BrainBeak; isn't she awesome? You can send a letter back with her to let us know you're okay and on your way.

See you soon,

Johnny

P.S. Don't let her land on your arm. Something about crushing your wrist bones to powder.

P.P.S. Don't look her directly in the eyes for more than two seconds.

P.P.P.S. Don't say anything to her that contains the letter "D"; it sets her off.

P.P.P.P.S. Don't breathe on or around her.

P.P.P.P.P.S. Don't show her any fear or uncertainty. Also don't express too many opinions.

P.P.P.P.P.P.S. Have fun!

13

PEONI TALKS
TO A STRANGER
IN THE WOODS

In which Peoni does something
that you should never do!

Peoni could still see the boys leaping down the mountainside like a couple of overzealous goats off to eat a pile of tin cans. This was exactly what she was afraid of. Exactly why she tried to do the tea ceremony on her own. They were taking her adventure and making it theirs.

Some inner voice told her that Joey and Johnny didn't mean to do it. They were just helping. They were her friends, and let's face it—she really wasn't doing that great on her own. Weren't there still a million steps and rules to learn? She better just buckle down and—

"Shut up, inner voice," she warned.

Joey and Johnny even got a cool riddle, and the wiseman didn't just tell it to them. He had a whole production surrounding it, all mysterious and weird. Awesome quest stuff. What'd she get? Some advice whispered in her ear that she already knew. And even *that* seemed to be about them.

So it was with lackluster effort that Peoni made her way back to Kick Foot Academy, stomping heavily through the woods in a very non-ninja way. To fit her mood she took gloomy pleasure in purposely stepping on dry sticks, and generally making as much noise as possible. So she was taken aback—something she rarely experienced—when a man stepped out from behind a tree.

"Hello," he said.

"Um, hello?" Peoni said back to him.

The man staring at her was whip-thin and quick-looking even while standing perfectly still. His eyes and mustache appeared to be battling each other for dominance over his face. If it was possible to see past those two features you might notice he was handsome.

He spoke quickly, displaying his open, empty

hands. "I know it might be a little startling to bump into a strange man in the middle of the woods, but I—"

Peoni cut him off. "I'm not afraid."

"Good, because—"

Peoni bent and picked something off the ground. She held the object between her fingers so he could see it. "I'm a ninja," she warned. "I can think of five ways to knock you out with this acorn. Are you a pirate?"

"It's the boots, isn't it?" They were big and brown, with large open cuffs at the top. He also had an expertly tailored shirt with billowing loose sleeves and a cut deep across the chest to show the top of a tattoo.

"You've got sea legs," Peoni stated. "I'm pretty good at recognizing katas, and I can tell you're used to standing on the deck of a ship."

"Well spotted." He smiled and his mustache smiled with him. "I'm Captain Captain Cornelius Loon, at your service." He tipped an invisible hat toward her.

"Aren't you a little far from water?"

"Aren't *you* a little nosy?" he teased. "I'm an ambassador. Ninjas and pirates have

5 WAYS TO KNOCK SOMEONE OUT WITH AN ORDINARY ACORN

1. Ricochet acorn off tree and into their temple.
2. Bribe squirrel to drop heavy branch on their head.
3. Throw down throat while they are talking.
4. Grind in powder. Make acorn-based knockout drug.
5. Throw high into air. Punch them in face while they are busy watching the acorn.

been at odds for far too long. I come to soothe the troubled waters between our two people."

While it was stated in this very book that the war between ninjas and pirates has been exaggerated, Peoni was willing to listen. After all, she was good friends with Johnny. Johnny hated pirates. He hated them with a cartoony passion. Maybe it was the tiny island he grew up on, or maybe it was simply because he was Johnny.

Peoni smiled. "So you decided to just wait in the woods, until you bumped into a ninja? Talk about Uncle Creepy."

He let loose a good-natured chuckle. "Nonsense, I was approaching your school when I heard you coming.

I was going to present myself to the great FangSwan, but perhaps you'd do even better."

That sentence was dangerously close to saying Peoni was better than FangSwan. The mere concept made her feel giddy. She had doubted that anybody was better at anything than FangSwan. This was, of course, ridiculous. For example, Peoni was far better at being a girl than FangSwan, and almost everyone was better at *not* killing people.

FangSwan was so good at being ninja, it made you question if there was anything he couldn't do. He once defeated a challenger by making precise strikes on the man's nerve clusters. This caused the man to punch himself in the face with his right hand while writing a letter of apology with his left.

It was probably for the best that Cornelius hadn't met FangSwan. For a pirate, Peoni thought, he seemed nice enough, and he probably liked his bones and skin right where they were.

"Why me?" Peoni asked.

"Why not you?" Cornelius answered. "I was wondering if you would fancy a spot of tea?"

"What did you say?" Peoni still didn't trust the man, but this was starting to sound like the adventure she had been hoping for.

"Tea! What better way to celebrate the start of new things? Come, join me. And together we'll take the first step toward pirates and ninjas becoming friends."

Peoni tossed the acorn over her shoulder and took the offered hand. The pirate captain thumped twice on the tree next to him and a rope ladder descended from the thick foliage above. Pirates in tree houses? This was sounding more like one of the boys' idiot adventures by the moment. Now she just needed some kind of—

"Oh!" Wonder filled Peoni's eyes as she climbed into the leaves.

"Captains," Cornelius announced, "I'd like to introduce you to our new friend, Peoni. Now someone fire up the kettle."

Peoni's mind raced back to the advice the wiseman had given her, and for the first time, it made her happy.

"Trust your friends."

WISEMAN NOTE: Other than frostbite, this is an example of the biggest risk in the mystical advice business. Even when you give the advice as clearly as you can, in the long run everyone has to figure it out for themselves.

14

WOW TOWER

In which the "wow"
is less about the tower.

Joey and Johnny met Knight-Lite the next day in Wow Tower Park. It was a city block full of trees, reflecting pools, and marble statues of very important, forgotten people. Joey and Johnny walked along a cobblestone pathway, their ninja toe socks making no sound. Parkgoers and giggling picnickers passed by them without a second glance while the sun blazed merrily above, looking very pleased with itself.

From the center of the park rose the alabaster splendor of Wow Tower, home of Lemming Falls's most beloved superhero.

Coming in a close second place for that honor, the armored duo of Night-Knight and Knight-Lite came screeching up to the ninjas on what appeared to be the seamless union of robotic horse and motorcycle. The vehicles blew up a dusty swirl from the two broad discs that held them floating inches off the ground.

Night-Knight's horse was huge and gray, and steam shot from its nostrils as the engine powered down. The overlapping metal plates covering its titanium frame were riveted together for strength rather than style. You could see evidence of past battles in the scarred metal.

Knight-Lite's was more of a hover-pony. It would've looked at home floating in a kiddie pool. It was light blue and shiny, with the oversize facial features of a smiling cartoon horse. It had a freshly painted look about it. The rear flank was branded with the graphic of a friendly dragon. Where Night-Knight's engine

thrummed with power, the sidekick's idled with a pleasant *putt-putt* sound. Joey did his levelheaded best not to roll his eyes as Knight-Lite wobbled his way off the hover-horse, got back to his feet, and dusted himself off.

The sidekick lifted the visor to his helmet. "I call her Dragonfly!"

"I love how you squealed the tires," Johnny said. "You don't even *have* tires!"

"Yeah, I found the sound effect on TwitFace and hooked it up to the speakers. Night-Knight made me take out the *VROOooom VROOooom* noises though."

The armored superhero cleared his throat loudly. "Maybe if it wasn't just you making the noise with your mouth . . . Now, if you're quite done introducing your friends to your *horse* . . ."

"Oh, sorry. Joey and Johnny, this is Night-Knight."

The hero swung his leg up and over the worn leather saddle, landing before the two ninjas with a powerful grace. "Wonderful to finally meet you both." His voice was a bit gravelly but with a distinct British accent. The boys experienced an odd moment of déjà vu, accompanied by another flurry of winking from Knight-Lite.

"Hello, sir," the boys said, trying to keep shaking awe out of their voices.

"I hear you need help planning a tea party," Night-Knight said.

Joey looked a little embarrassed. "It's a lot more ninja than it sounds."

Superheroes and ninjas do not traditionally get along. Night-Knight was one of the exceptions. Sure, he seemed like a superhero. The Knight was broad-shouldered, tall, and heavily muscled, with a heroically deep voice. Like most of his friends, he too dressed in spandex and wore his underpants on the outside. His enemies included everything from Space Tyrants to Robotic Squid. Night-Knight had all the hallmarks of a superhero, and yet there was something so very . . . *ninja* about him.

Though armed with gadgets, Night-Knight possessed no superpowers, and he routinely proved he didn't need them. Despite being surrounded by beings who could eat diamonds and see through time, this "normal" human remained one of the most effective and prominent heroes in the city. In fact, the only hero who even held a candle to him was the man they were going to see today.

"Captain Wow," Knight-Lite said as they approached the hero's headquarters. "Golly, he's got this amazing computer system. It's made of crystals and space stuff—it's the best."

"*Second*-best." Night-Knight glanced down at his sidekick. "Unfortunately the Armory's system is down for *some reason.*"

Knight-Lite took two stumbling steps forward before catching himself. "I, um . . . had trouble downloading the latest compatibility patch?" he squeaked.

"For what?"

"Stuff?"

Inside Wow Tower's main lobby the group was greeted by robots. They welcomed everyone, made offers of refreshment, and escorted them to the elevators.

"Did you see that open tube next to the elevator?" Johnny asked. "That's because Captain Wow can fly."

"It's a safety hazard," Joey declared, "that's what that is."

"If *we ninjas* oversleep five minutes, people shoot at us with arrows."

Joey took his eye off the advancing floor numbers. "Your point?"

"Safety isn't one of your big concerns. Joey . . . are you jealous?"

"I'm not jealous," Joey whispered, really wishing they weren't having this conversation in front of the Knights. "It's just a little unfair. I mean, we train every day and he's just born with space powers?" Joey mimed holding something huge over his head. "'Hi, I'm from Neptune. Where would you like me to put this dump truck?'"

Night-Knight coughed, covering a sound that might have been a snort of laughter.

"I know some heroes are like that," Knight-Lite said, "but not the Captain. You'll see. He's constantly looking out for the city, and he always saves every lemming at the Lemming Drop Festival."

When the elevator doors opened, they found Captain Wow floating ten feet in the air as he pulled and prodded at a collection of wires sprouting from a constantly beeping box. At his waist hung a tool belt filled with unrecognizable gizmos. He floated down as he saw them enter, leaving the box to its incessant beeping.

"Greetings!" he declared with wide welcoming arms.

The Captain had short, dirty-blond hair and a chiseled jawline. His powerful frame sported a dazzling collection of muscles, which rippled under his skintight blue-and-white uniform. The cape was new, a gift from the city after saving the theater district from the League of Evil Critics.

"Good to see you, Knight-Lite!" he said, giving the squire a smack on the shoulder that nearly crumpled him to the floor. He pointed a thumb at the box above them. "You mind giving the Para-Stalitic-Anti-Neurilizer a little look? Can't get the thing to stop yelling at me!"

"No, sir, I can't!" replied Knight-Lite.

Joey and Johnny looked shocked; they'd never seen their friend miss an opportunity to be helpful, and Captain Wow didn't seem like a man anyone could refuse. The Captain just cocked his head and gave the tiny knight a quizzical look.

"I can't look at your Para-Stalitic-Anti-Neurilizer because you just made that word up! But I *will* look at your Analid-Trans-Positronic Conversion Processor!" chirped Knight-Lite with a look of pure delight.

"Ha!" Captain Wow guffawed so explosively it spun Joey's mask around. "Can't pull one over on our Li'l Tin Technician, can I?" He handed some kind of cosmic wrench to Knight-Lite, who clicked his shoes into a hover platform and rose up to

127

happily tinker with the annoying box.

Captain Wow turned his attention to the two ninjas. "Joey, Johnny—a pleasure." The Captain's smile bathed them in a warm glow as he shook their hands. "And Joey," he said with a wink, "I come from Planet 80, not Neptune."

A ninja mask can conceal many things, but Joey's flush of embarrassment was not one of them.

Night-Knight rode to the rescue, engaging the good Captain in superheroic matters. Checking on who'd been captured, who'd escaped, who'd been mutated into a monster by gamma rays.

With a few quick twists of wire and two minutes of tapping away on his wrist keyboard, Knight-Lite not only ended the irritating beeping, he also managed to get Captain Wow seven more TV channels from his home galaxy. The Captain turned on a wall-size view screen and they all watched as a blue liquid blob burped at a greenish blob. "Ah, I saw this episode as a kid!" he said, pointing with excitement at the screen. "This is when Flar-Whoop and Plexicon Twelve have to perform a dance for Habberspoodles Day but they accidentally bring a Gersimian bush instead of the traditional Bargerygump shrub!" He snorted at their obvious foolishness.

Captain Wow insisted on a celebration. With a single button press, robots rolled out from hidden slots in the walls, each carrying a tray piled high with sandwiches, cookies, and drinks.

"What about EyeFace?" asked Night-Knight. He still wore his helmet and had to awkwardly sip his coffee through a straw.

"Haven't heard a peep, which makes me think he's up to something," Captain Wow replied, popping another tiny cucumber sandwich in his mouth.

"The Captain even baked the cookies into the shapes of little ninjas," Johnny said. "How cool is that?" He broke off a cookie sword, carefully replacing it with a toothpick and cheese cube. The end result *sort* of looked like a hammer. If you squinted.

As the heroes continued to speak, Knight-Lite beckoned the boys to follow him. He pulled them down a corridor and into a white room that held only a single hovering crystal in the center. In a hushed, excited whisper, he said, "I tapped into Captain Wow's Holotube while I was up there!"

"You DID?" mumbled Joey

through a mouthful of ninja cookie. "Well, that's just . . . wow, his Holo-tube! So . . . great!"

"That's exactly how I like my, uh, tubes!" said Johnny. "As hollow as possible!"

Knight-Lite snorted in exasperation. "Guys, it's basically a 3D TV."

"Ooooooh!" said Joey. "You mean to help us figure out the riddle?"

"No, to watch the 1983 *RabbitShark! Holiday! Special!*" Knight-Lite's smile could not be contained.

"You mean the one that only aired once and that even the creators tried to bury?" Joey asked. Since Johnny had brought the 1980s television show to the group last year, they had all become experts. Whether or not they loved the show was irrelevant.

"Y-you-you-you . . ." Johnny was beyond speech. He hugged the sidekick to him like a long-lost brother. Finally released from the embrace of a moist-eyed Johnny, Knight-Lite began fiddling with MERLIN— his wrist-mounted gadget that served as both shield and web browser.

"Night-Knight's Armory might have a better computer, but Wow's got way sharper graphics."

The crystal glowed, creating a curtain of light and then, before their eyes, the 1983 *RabbitShark Holiday Special* began to play in glorious 3D. Joey opened wide and bit the head off another ninja.

"Melting ice caps? That does explain why there's always a body of water everywhere they go," Johnny said.

"I can't believe it had three musical numbers," Joey moaned. "And what, exactly, were the Fin Friends Five?"

Knight-Lite piped up eagerly. "That was the series' attempt to generate a spin-off show. Each of the five had a different aquatic pal, but every show still generally ended up with the bad guy getting eaten by a different fish."

"That must've been really upsetting to watch when it was a piranha," Joey said. "I mean, it was just one piranha. They're tiny."

The heroes had wrapped up whatever they were talking about and rejoined the boys. Captain Wow looked like he had to remind himself to touch the ground between steps. Night-Knight pretended annoyance, but it had been nice to take the time to actually enjoy his cup of coffee. As much as you *can* enjoy coffee through a straw.

"So if you're all done watching the telly, the Captain and I think we might have a solution to some of your problems."

Captain Wow hovered to the window, gesturing far below.

"My neighbor Ms. Carbunkle might be able to help," he said. "She lives right on the edge of the park. Nice old lady."

"Sir," asked Joey hopefully, "do you maybe know of

any multi-armed, hulking trolls we could steal the tea from? Or perhaps an army of lobster-men?"

"Well yeah," said Captain Wow, sounding a little confused. "I know plenty of lobster-men, trolls too, but none of them can make a cup of tea like Ms. Carbuncle. Hers is the best I've ever had, and I've been to space!"

"So . . . ," Joey pondered, "they've got good tea in space?"

"Oh yeah, it's the best."

Night-Knight patted his squire on the shoulder. "In the meantime, Knight-Lite can assist you from the armory. He really knows his way around a keyboard. Narrow down the search on those other clues, get back to you in a couple of days."

"Did you say *he*?" asked Knight-Lite.

"What?"

"You said *he*!"

"Well . . . I . . . aren't you . . . ?"

"I'm a *girl*!!" bawled Knight-Lite.

There was a *whoosh* sound as four sets of eyebrows shot upward simultaneously.

"What? Since when?" sputtered Night-Knight.

"Since always!" Knight-Lite put her face in her hand in disbelief. "My name is Lindsay. Lindsay Lightheart."

"World's greatest detective, huh?" Captain Wow muttered.

Night-Knight rallied. "Lindsay can be a boy's name."

Knight-Lite turned on Joey and Johnny. "I've been his squire for almost two years! Can you believe this?!"

"Well, actually," began Johnny, "we didn't know—"

"What a lovely girl you would turn out to be!" finished Joey, giving Johnny a little shin kick.

Captain Wow took the opportunity to corral Joey and Johnny toward the elevator. His jaw was still clenched as he battled the forces of laughter. "I'm sure this will work itself out," he said, "but it's probably best if we just make a quiet exit. Go talk to Ms. Carbunkle." Neither Knight noticed Captain Wow leaving, despite the fact that he was six foot six and wearing a bright blue cape. Neither did they notice Joey or Johnny, but . . . they're ninjas.

"The girl thing . . . did *you* know?" Captain Wow asked after the elevator doors closed behind them.

"We just thought she was a boy who liked to smell nice," Johnny said.

WISEMAN NOTE: Um . . . I honestly did NOT see that one coming.

15

LAWN LAVA

In which Joey and Johnny heroically
cross a pleasant lawn on a nice day.
Does it always have to be explosions
and dragons?

Joey eyed the vast expanse of vivid green grass
that stretched between Wow Tower and their
destination. They could see the tiny, cozy house in
the distance. Perhaps there was mortal danger lurk-
ing in the dappled shade from the trees lining the tidy
brick pathway? Maybe the feathery birds would try to
skewer them with their joyously chirping beaks? The
skittering chipmunks certainly seemed to have cheeky
expressions on their fat faces. Were they thinking evil
thoughts? Possibly, but probably not. It was a really,
really nice day out. It was a day made for fountains and

picnics—evil would be hard to come by.

Joey made an explosion noise and spoke in the voice of a man doing a movie trailer. "Joey and Johnny, the ninjas!" He swung his arm through the air. He could almost see their names appearing above their heads in letters of fire. "Watch as they stroll through a park on a delightful sunny day!" Explosion sound. "Can they make it to the old lady's house and borrow some tea?" Bigger explosion sound. "Will they get a LEMON COOKIE?!"

"Joey, you are looking at this all wrong," Johnny said. "Remember that book by Arugalla Picklebee that I lent you? We need to be like the characters in *Pretending to Be Meatballs*. Spiffel and Plork learned how to use their imaginations to have great adventures."

"Johnny, every book you lend me makes me worry about that woman. Spiffel and Plork used their imaginations to turn into meatballs and were thrown into a stewpot at the end!"

"Ugh," said Johnny, remembering. "Man, Arugalla sure has a hard time with happy endings." He slapped Joey on the shoulder. "But we can pretend something better!" Johnny jumped into a tree, shouting, "The lawn is lava!"

Joey rolled his eyes and grunted, but since he didn't want to burn his feet on lava, he followed Johnny up the tree.

They leapt from branch to branch, flipping through the leaves, scattering birds and chipmunks in their wake. The boys had no way of knowing it, but the chipmunks were indeed thinking evil thoughts. It was chipmunk evil, though, so not much to be concerned about. Even a really well-thrown nut doesn't hurt that much.

When the trees ran out, Joey vaulted toward the pathway he thought was lava-free, but behind him Johnny yelled, "No! Wait! Now the path is lava and the lawn is safe!"

"Gah!" yelled Joey as he desperately readjusted in midflight. One foot touched lawn, but he was off-balance and leaning backward toward the path. He flailed, clawing for invisible ropes. But since the invisible ropes didn't exist, he was doomed to fall back into the lava.

WISEMAN NOTE: Which also didn't exist.

Moments before Joey was turned into a smoldering ruin, Johnny flipped from his tree, snagged Joey's arm, and pulled him back to safety.

"Whew," said Johnny, wiping an arm across his brow. "That was close."

"Johnny, I really don't think this is—"

"Shut up, Joey. This is totally working! It really appears we're on an adventure."

A series of small silver nozzles erupted from the ground with a metallic *ka-chink*. Johnny bounced to his feet. "It's . . . um . . . danger nozzles! . . . No, uh . . . laser bee dispensers . . ."

"Acid, Johnny! They spray acid!" said Joey, already flipping between the spurting streams of water from the lawn sprinklers.

"Oh! Good one." Johnny flipped and dodged as well, but the speed of his third spin was just slightly off. His right leg was sprinkled on. "AAAAAARRRGH!"

Joey turned as his friend screamed. Johnny had collapsed, holding his leg. A few passing joggers gave them odd looks.

"Nooooooo!" said Joey, turning back.

"Go, Joey!" gasped Johnny. ". . . My . . . my leg. It's been slightly dampened! . . . There is no hope . . . for me."

Joey ran to his friend's side. The sprinklers retracted, their evil work completed. Birds still sang, but the song was no longer joyous. To the boys they now twittered a melancholy dirge.

"You get up, Johnny! It's not over yet!" Joey checked Johnny's leg and winced; it was indeed slightly damp. "You crazy fool! Don't give up on me. You're the bravest darn ninja I ever met."

"Is . . . is that you, Joey? The world is going dark! I can no longer remember the taste of pancakes . . .

Tell . . . tell Peoni I . . . I think her spiky hair is pretty cool."

"No, Johnny! You're gonna tell her yourself. And you're going to eat pancakes while doing it! I may not be able to give you a dry pant leg, but darn it all, I *can* carry you!" With a defiant roar, Joey threw his friend across his shoulders.

"No . . . leave me, I'd probably just spit crumbs into her face when I talk," Johnny said.

Joey pointed in front of them. "Look, there's the house. That old lady can probably cure you."

"She has to be a witch named Moldybones, or I'm just gonna stay here and finish my death scene."

"Moldybones?"

"Let's face it, Joey, I'm better at making up names than you."

They came to the tidy white gate that separated Ms. Carbunkle from the rest of the world. In every way, the house that stood before them looked as cute as it was possible for a structure to look. It had white shutters with tiny red painted flowers. Ivy grew along the powder-blue siding. The roof was a bustle of perfectly arranged shingles and even the gutters were so charming you wanted to call them something other than "gutters." Maybe "water trestles" . . . no, I'll have to work on it, but "gutters" is just awful.

"Monkey flops! That's a witch's house! Moldybones is for *real*!" Johnny yelled, clambering off Joey's shoulders.

"Oh, come on, this is already getting confusing . . . I call time-out." Joey argued for logic, but he wouldn't have been entirely surprised to find a couple of lost German kids chewing on the house's cookie-like exterior. Other than one disturbingly aesthetic bird nest, the house was simply *too* clean. Like it had just been taken out of a box . . . or a candy wrapper.

Johnny was satisfied. "Yep, this is *so* a witch's house. I'm getting my hammer out."

"No, Johnny, put it away! We don't want to scare her." Joey tried to push the hammer back, but it was no use. Even if he could wrestle it away from his friend, there was no "back" to push it. He didn't know where Johnny pulled it from. . . . No one did.

WISEMAN NOTE: That is not strictly true.

"I think your imagination is stuck," Joey said, lunging after Johnny, who was waving his hammer at the door. "Try smacking your head a couple times!"

"Not when there's a witch about. Get behind me; I'll try to ward her off!"

"I said, *time-out!*" Joey leapt onto Johnny, and the two of them rolled across the perfectly manicured grass. "We are on a quest to get tea from an old lady. It might be the lamest quest ever, but we are not going to fail because YOU think she's a—"

There was a noise behind them. Locks were being unlocked, chains unchained, latches unlatched, and

hooks unhooked. The front door swung open. The little old lady on the other side peered out. She fixed her eyes on Johnny. "What are you kids doing on my lawn?"

"See?" said Johnny, gesturing toward the woman. "There is a psychic bond between witches and their lawns."

"What did he just—"

Joey stepped between Johnny and Ms. Carbunkle with his hands clasped in front of him like a friendly salesman. He knew his ninja mask covered his winning smile, so Joey blinked as adorably as he could. "Ma'am, we're so sorry to disturb you, but—"

"Ninjas, eh?" She sniffed. "I don't want any kung foos, young man, so you just take your karate chops and sell them elsewhere!"

"We're not selling kung foos, ma'am, we were hoping to—"

"Well, I'm not pledging my soul to the tentacles of the ten-thousand-eyed goat either, so take your pamphlets to Mr. Henderson across the street. He's into that sort of thing."

Joey was quickly losing control of the situation.

"No. Wait!" The door was closing in his face. He had been trained in a dozen ways to kick it down, but right now that just didn't seem a very ninja thing to do. "Your neighbor, Captain Wow, sent us!"

"Oh, the fella in blue-and-white pajamas? He is such a nice young man! He mows my lawn with his laser beam eyes, you know!"

"Uh, yeah, he's pretty great," Joey said.

"He lightly scorched my azaleas the last time, though. I'm going to have to bring that up at the next neighborhood meeting." She looked them up and down. "Hmmm, well . . . I guess you boys could come in for a cup of tea."

"Thank you, ma'am," Joey said. After a quick elbow in the ribs, Johnny begrudgingly put back his hammer.

The hallway they entered smelled of flowers and old clocks. When Ms. Carbunkle closed the door the sunny day squeezed away until they were left in almost total darkness. The only light came from the dim glow of hundreds of glittering eyes. Behind them, there was the sound of the old woman securing the locks and chains.

Suddenly Joey had the distinct impression that even though there were no bones strewn by the entrance, they had just walked into something truly terrifying.

"Johnny," Joey whispered, "I think I owe you an apology."

16

A CHAT AND SOME TEA

In which something terrible
happens involving pianos.

"Oh, I'm sorry, boys, I should probably turn on some lights for you. I get so used to the darkness."

"You . . . you mean the darkness in your soul, Moldybones?" Johnny replied to the creaky voice floating from the pitch black.

"Who now?" As she moved the glowing eyes shifted, rocking lightly back and forth, assessing the two ninjas.

"Johnny, stop it."

"There we go," Ms. Carbunkle said. The weak yellowy lights snapped on, revealing a carpeted hallway lined with flowery wallpapered walls. The eyes that had pinpricked the dark like stars belonged to

Ms. Carbunkle's impressive collection of cats. They swished their tails with expressions that ranged from disdainful to even more disdainful.

"Why don't you boys take your shoes off and come inside?"

"We'd love to take our shoes off, ma'am, but it would involve taking our pants off, too," Joey said.

"Oh dear, we can't have that," she said, handing each of them a towel and a bottle of spray cleaner. "Just give your feet a good scrubbing then."

They dutifully did as they were told. "This is *so* not ninja," Joey mumbled to himself as they followed Ms. Carbunkle into the next room, leaving a trail of flower-scented footprints behind them.

"You boys sit right there, I'll go get the kettle on." She gestured to a plush sofa. The plastic squeaked underneath them as they sat down. "You can have a nice little talkie with the babies," she said as she walked into the kitchen.

Eight of the babies stepped out of the shadows and followed them into the living room. They stationed themselves at various points around the sofa, each with a very important job to do. Two went to work sharpening their claws on Joey's legs. Another peered at him from over the arm of the sofa, giving Joey's hand an occasional whack for no apparent reason. A big bruiser of a cat with a torn ear sat in his lap and maintained unblinking eye contact. The remaining four took position behind Johnny's head and had an intensely serious game of tetherball with his dooley-bopper.

"... and there we are," Ms. Carbunkle said as she bustled back into the room with a tray piled high with teacups and cookies. "Do you like lemon cookies?"

Joey shot a sideways glance at Johnny. With a pained expression he said, "Yes, ma'am, we both like lemon cookies." Joey made a motion to help with the tray, but the bruiser cat's eyes hadn't yet given him permission to move, so he just sat quietly as Ms. Carbunkle served them. Johnny held his head stiffly in hopes of not making his dooley-bopper do anything "fun."

"So what did Mister Wow send you for?" asked Ms. Carbunkle as she settled onto the chair across from them. It was difficult to hear her over the drone of purring that had arisen since she entered the room.

"Well, ma'am," Joey practically shouted, "we need to get some spirit tea! By chance would you have some we could borrow?"

"Oh deary, you can't borrow tea!" said the old woman. Joey and Johnny's heads fell slightly. "But I'd be willing to trade you for some chores! What can you boys do?" The steam rising from her teacup fogged her glasses, hiding her eyes from view.

"Well, we can infiltrate an enemy stronghold in deadly silence and eradicate a tyrannical despotic shogun for you!" said Joey hopefully.

"I can hit things with my hammer so hard they turn into a gas," added Johnny.

Feeling that she was unmoved, Joey added, "Oh! I can build a hang glider, and Johnny can explain every episode of RabbitShark."

"I'll do that for free." Johnny smiled.

"Mr. Flandershots still hasn't returned my lasagna pan . . . ," offered Ms. Carbunkle.

"Yes!" Johnny stood, gripping his hammer. He used it to pulverize the teacup in his other hand. "Where is this villain, Mr. Flandershots? We shall retrieve your lasagna pan, ma'am!"

"Young man, you just broke my teacup and dripped tea on my sofa!" Ms. Carbunkle rose from her chair, spilling a pile of cats onto the floor. "I better get a dishcloth before it stains the plastic!"

"Sorry, ma'am." Johnny sat down, but stood up quickly before the tea could soak his pants. One of the cats lunged widely for his dooley-bopper. Ms. Carbunkle came back with a rag to clean the mess and then handed Johnny a fresh cup of tea, this time served in a plastic sippy cup with cartoon bunnies on it. Johnny slurped his tea through the straw and mumbled his thanks.

"I don't know any shoguns, and on second thought I can't send ninjas after Mr. Flandershots. He writes letters." She shuddered at this. "And I'm pretty sure I have enough gas."

"Well . . ." Joey was feeling at a loss. His legs were also falling asleep, but every time he shifted them the bruiser would extend his claws just enough to change Joey's mind.

"I suppose you could move my pianos."

It was no shogun, but Joey realized moving a couple of pianos was a bargain. It could be done in no time and they could then get on with an activity more befitting their dangerous lifestyle. "Done!" said Joey. He squeezed his eyes shut against bruiser cat's penetrating stare and stood up. It earned him a long tear down his pant leg.

Johnny stood as well and bent his head toward Joey. "Are you sure, Joey? If we don't lift with our legs, we could hurt our backs."

Joey was grumbling and trying to use a ninja star to pin his pant leg closed. "I'm sure we can move a couple of pianos, Johnny!"

"Oh, it's not a couple, deary," Ms. Carbunkle said as she led them upstairs. "I have one piano for every year of my life."

Johnny clutched Joey's shoulder. "Joey! How are we going to move FIVE HUNDRED PIANOS?"

BROKEN GIRAFFES

In which Scar Eyeface does something that seems nice but probably isn't.

Scar EyeFace was holding a ceramic giraffe leg in his hand. He stared at it and frowned. "Joey," he said. The buzz saw screamed to life for a few moments. "Johnny." The saw roared once more. He'd been doing this for several hours, all while staring intently at the spindly leg.

There was a knock on the door.

"Who is it?" he said, his eyes still fixed on the leg.

"Tim, sir!" came a voice from the other side.

"That's not very helpful," growled Scar EyeFace.

"Tim from special information, sir!"

EyeFace opened the door by poking the button with a hoof. Tim walked in carrying a clipboard stuffed to bursting with messily written notes.

"What do you have for me, Tim from special information?"

"Uh, you asked about the two ninjas, sir. They just left the old woman's house . . ."

"What are they doing now?"

"Deciding on where to have lunch."

Scar EyeFace started to laugh. Tim looked down at his feet because it was Evil Laugh Number 37. It was the one he used when he was about to push his trapdoor button. Tim shuffled to the left.

"This is too perfect, Tim!"

"Um, yes, sir."

"Let's get the boys some lunch!"

"Really, sir? Lunch?"

"Oh yes, we're going to send them to meet the waiter!"

Tim trembled and dropped his clipboard in a clatter. Notes scattered across the floor. "Oh, uh, sir! That hardly seems necessary, couldn't we . . . it just seems . . . they're so young!"

"Make it happen, Tim, or next time I'll buy *you* lunch!"

Tim stifled a sob, gathered up his notes, and slunk out the door. Scar EyeFace went back to staring at the leg.

"Joey," he said, and the saw roared to life.

THE WAITER

In which . . . it's too upsetting,
can we just not talk about it?

"I never want to see a piano again," Johnny moaned. Two days after walking through the front door, a couple of bruised, aching ninjas limped out of Ms. Carbunkle's house. Ten minutes later Joey and Johnny stood on a busy street corner. For their trouble Johnny carried a small package of tea clutched loosely in one hand, a bag of lemon cookies in the other.

"I never want to see another lemon cookie," Joey said.

"Then don't look in the bag."

"Why did you take them?"

"I was sooooooo hungry, Joey, but I just can't do it," Johnny almost sobbed. "We've eaten nothing but lemon cookies for two days. She's some kind of *monster*!" He wheezed and threw the bag into the next trash can they passed.

Neither of the ninjas could say just how many pianos they had moved. They'd both stopped counting somewhere around number fifty-nine. That was the one where Joey had forgotten to lift with his legs.

"Oh man, my back!" Joey said, trying to straighten but getting only about halfway. "How did a single-story house have *seven* staircases?"

Johnny grabbed his complaining stomach. "I'm dying, Joey. I gotta eat. NOW!"

Joey agreed. He found a reasonably clean sheet of paper in the garbage and used his camouflage kit to write "Will Ninja for Food!" on it. He held it up between the two of them while they each did their best to look as visible as possible. Neither of the boys had actually tried to be *in*visible, but sometimes being ninja is hard to turn off. It took less time than they thought, but more than Johnny had hoped.

"Excuse me, are you boys ninjas?" A man popped out of the crowd and peered at them with a sweaty face and nervous, shifting eyes.

Joey pointed at his ninja mask. "Yes, we are!"

The nervous guy thrust two red coupons at him. "Here, take them! They're good for two free lunches at Lemming Falls's world-famous Snooty'Garbeux's Food'splosion and Eatery."

Johnny gasped in delight. "Snooty'Garbeux's! That's the best restaurant ever."

"What do we have to do for them?" asked Joey, eyeing the coupons suspiciously.

"Nothing!" said the man. "Just ask for . . ." He sobbed a little before continuing, "Ask for table seven."

"We're not taking anything for free; we have to do something ninja for you in return."

"Oh, come on, Joey," cried Johnny. "I'm dying!"

"*We're doing something ninja for the man!*" Joey insisted.

The nervous guy looked around. "Uh, fine . . . um . . ." He pointed at a man passing by. "That guy stole my car keys!"

Joey held up a hand with a pair of keys dangling from them. "You mean *these* keys?" The wide grin under his mask went completely unnoticed.

"Yeah! Great! Amazing! Enjoy lunch!" The man shoved the coupons at Joey. He almost forgot to grab the keys. Before fading back into the crowd he turned and said in a shaky voice, "Remember, ask for table seven!"

"And *that*," said Joey, slapping his hands together, "is how a ninja earns himself some lunch."

"Yeah!" said Johnny. "Plus we thwarted a dastardly car-key thief!"

Joey and Johnny walked through the richly carved doorway of Snooty'Garbeux's and stood politely in front of the maître d'. A commotion in the back of the restaurant currently had the man's full attention. He was shouting to his staff in French, and some were shouting back in a mixture of French and heavily accented English. The only words Joey caught were *paramedics* and *'urry!*

Joey politely coughed into his fist, earning him a look from the large man.

"Err, wat can I due for you bouyz?" the maître d' said in between looks over his shoulder and more shouting.

"We've come for lunch," said Joey.

The man gave the two boys a looking over. His sharp eyes paused for a long moment on Joey's pant leg with the ninja star holding it together. He also stopped on Johnny's dooley-bopper, but who doesn't?

"Eer, no!" he said, waving his arm at them. "You 'ave come to ze wrong place! Go down ze road to ze park, zer iz a man there who laks to feed ze peegeons! He will give you bread!" The maître d' turned back to his commotion and continued to shout.

Johnny smashed a potted plant with his hammer, earning him a few more moments of the maître d's attention.

"Mr. Smashy says we're having lunch here!" Johnny said, holding his hammer close to his ear so that it could whisper things to him.

Joey held up the two red coupons. "Forgive my friend. We have only eaten cookies for the last two days. We were told to ask for table seven."

The effect on the maître d' was instantaneous; his eyes grew wide and soft. He stifled a sob as he said, "Wah? You bouyz? Table seven? But . . . you ar' so young!"

"Mr. Smashy notices that you have more potted plants . . . ," said Johnny.

The man wiped a tear from his eye and nodded. "I will seet you gentleman in wan moment, of course!" He shouted to his staff again. Some of them gave Joey and Johnny the same wide-eyed, sad look. A few shook their heads and looked away. "Your table iz just being cleared." He gave Joey a gentle pat on the shoulder.

The source of the commotion soon became apparent as a gurney was wheeled toward them. It was surrounded by paramedics shouting instructions to one another. There were beeping machines and hoses everywhere. A man with a video camera ran alongside, recording the proceedings with great enthusiasm. He shouted excitedly to the man on the gurney, "If you survive, this is going to be some great TV, Mr. Jurgen, sir!" There was no sign of acknowledgment.

Joey grabbed Johnny by the shoulder and pointed at the approaching group. "Johnny! I think that's Yeager Jurgen."

"Which one?" asked Johnny.

"The guy lying down covered in the horribly stained sheet."

The man was indeed famous survivalist Yeager Jurgen, and the sheet he was under was truly stained horribly. If it's any comfort at all, most of the terrible stains were from a variety of soups and sauces. The stains that weren't soup or sauce were . . . oh, let's just call them *all* soup and sauce stains, shall we? He also seemed to have a collection of cutlery poking out from various spots on his prone form, a portion of squid tentacle wrapped around his neck, and huge shark's teeth jutting from the spots that weren't already occupied by cutlery. He didn't look too good.

Joey couldn't contain himself. He ran to the gurney and shouted at Yeager's face. "I'm your biggest fan, sir! Do you remember me from the book signing last fall? Can I please have another autograph?" He looked around the room for something to sign. "Excuse me, is there anything here Mr. Jurgen can head-butt for me?"

"Hey, kid!" shouted the paramedic who was

searching for a pulse on Yeager's wrist. "No auto-graphs!"

"Oh no," said Joey, looking crestfallen. "Is this a new policy?"

"Uh, yeah, he's got a policy against signing autographs while dead." The man's sarcasm went right over Joey's head and withered the potted plant behind him.

"Mr. Jurgen's not dead," said Joey. "He's a professional survivalist!"

"Guess we'll see about that." The paramedic yanked a shark's tooth out of Yeager's leg and tossed it to Joey. "There's yer autograph, buddy!"

Joey caught the tooth and proudly held it up for Johnny to see. "Look at that. There's even a little soup stain at the tip!"

The maître d' waved to the departing gurney as it was loaded onto the ambulance outside. "Thank you, zir! Please come again . . . if you are able!"

From back in the dining area a man with a hazmat suit and a mop gave a thumbs-up to the maître d'. He turned to the boys and with a controlled sniffle said, "Zirs, your table ees ready! I yam so sorry."

Their table was at the back of the restaurant and hidden by a folding partition. While all the other tables had the tidy look of effortless perfection, table seven looked like it had been traumatized but was doing its best to act normal around its friends. The tablecloth looked clean at first glance, but any closer examination revealed hundreds of faded stains. The chairs were pockmarked with deep gouges, and patches crisscrossed the leather cushions. The carpet underneath their feet looked brand-new—in fact, it looked as though it had just been rolled out five minutes ago.

The maître d' handed them each a menu and gave them a last, long look through red-rimmed eyes. "Au revoir, you two innocent young angels! May you fly to heaven on ze wings of doves!"

"What do we need the doves for if we're angels?" asked Johnny.

"Is fine dining always this dramatic?" asked Joey.

"Your waiter will be with you zoon."

Pierre had wanted to be a waiter since birth. It was the reason his parents had named him Pierre. While other parents wished for their children to become doctors, lawyers, and ninja-book writers, Pierre's parents had the desperate hope that their son would be the sort of waiter the world would remember. His father had been a waiter all his life and had made the family fortune through tips alone. He would often take his son on walks around the family mansion and point out all the rich luxuries that his expert waitering had earned him. Pointing at the crystal chandelier, he would say, "*That,* my son, is because I served a perfect cup of coffee to the

Duke of Sainsbury!" Gesturing to the marble staircase, he'd say, "And *that* is for serving a cheesecake to the King of Prussia at *exactly* the right temperature!" There was nothing Pierre wanted more than to earn his parents' praise and become the world's greatest waiter.

But it didn't happen. Pierre was a terrible waiter. He was really, truly just an awful, awful waiter. I mean, WOW . . .

Pierre was so bad at waitering that it was extremely rare for one of his customers to survive past the salad course. Only three, including Yeager Jurgen, had ever made it to the entree. Now usually, this level of awful customer service would result in a fellow finding another line of work, perhaps as a teddy-bear stuffer or a pudding stirrer. In Pierre's case, his waitering abilities were merely utilized for an entirely different purpose. A darker purpose. A purpose that Pierre himself was completely unaware of.

Scar EyeFace put him to work at one of the many restaurants he owned and gave him his own table. If Mr. EyeFace had a problem that he wished to dispose of permanently, that problem was given a coupon for a free meal. At table seven.

Joey and Johnny had not even had a chance to look at the menus placed in front of them. If they had, they would have noticed that table seven had its own menu, complete with an embossed number seven on the cover. They might also have noticed that both menus looked beaten and dented like gladiators' shields. The boys didn't notice these details because they were still cleaning up from an issue with the water glasses. Joey had reached for his glass to take a sip when the thing shattered explosively, unleashing a torrent of water so hot it made the tablecloth smoke.

"Oh," said Joey, "it was boiling. . . . I thought the bubbles were because it was fancy."

Pierre opened the partition. He was holding a razor-sharp steak knife out in front of him. "'Allo! I yam Pierre, your . . ." His foot hit the edge of the carpet, sending him careening toward Joey, who was still carefully mopping up the boiling water. Joey flicked to the right, allowing the knife to bury itself in the deeply scarred wall by his head. "Oh zir! I yam zo zorry!" cried Pierre as he tried to pull the knife free. When he finally yanked the knife out, it slipped from his hand and hurtled toward Johnny.

Johnny caught the knife by the blade and handed it back to Pierre. "There you go, buddy. Those things'll get away from you sometimes."

"You 'ave no idea!" replied Pierre, immediately dropping the knife to the floor, where it quivered next to Joey's foot. "'Ave zirs enjoyed your gently warmed table water?"

"Uh, yeah, about that," said Joey, waving his hand around the still-smoking table. "That water was boiling, and generally one serves ice water with dinner."

Pierre was devastated by this news. He punched his own leg while shouting, "*Mon dieu!* I yam zo stupeed. Wat are you theenking, Pierre? It eez ice water, of course!" He left and came back within seconds carrying two new glasses that had smoke pouring from the top.

"Uh," said Joey, pointing at the smoking glasses, "I think those are also hot, Pierre."

"Ah! Zir, you are meestaken." Pierre looked very proud of himself. "Zis iz *dry* ice. She smokes but eez so very much colder!" This was proven when Pierre's flourish knocked over Johnny's glass, spilling it over the candelabra, which promptly shattered. "Only ze very coldest water for my two friends!"

Joey picked up his menu and moved his chair away from the gently crackling table. "I think we're ready to order, Pierre."

"Oh!" interrupted Johnny. "Let me order for us, Joey! I'm DYING to eat!!"

"Go for it, Johnny, but please stop saying that . . ."

Johnny eagerly glanced through his menu. "Ummm, how's the puffer-fish appetizer, Pierre?"

"Ah! Ze puffer fish, she eez almost completely poisonous, but I will expertly cut out for you and serve only ze deelicious part."

"Don't you just serve the fish, Pierre? Why are you doing the cooking too?" asked Joey.

"For zum reason they let me do thees part!"

"Two of those, please," said Johnny. "And for the salad we'll have theeee . . . wow, there's a Venus flytrap salad?! This place *is* fancy! Two of those . . ."

"Very good, zir, ze teeth zey are very beeg!"

"Well, I love big teeth in my salad, Pierre," said Joey, doing his best to look as though he understood fine dining.

"For the main course . . ." Johnny knitted his brows together in great concentration. "How fresh is the great white shark?"

"It eez quite surprisingly fresh. Mr. Jurgen, he seemed to lak eet very much . . ."

"Yeager Jurgen ate that?" cried Joey. "I'll have one of those!"

"No shark for me, Pierre," said Johnny. "Give me the flaming-skewers-of-meat platter, please. . . ."

"And ze dessert?"

"Death by chocolate, please," said Johnny, closing his menu.

"Um . . . ," said Joey, "I think I'll just have the pumpkin pie."

"Ah yes." Pierre nodded as he wrote down the order. "Death by pumpkin pie, very gud!"

From the other side of table seven's merciful partition, music was playing. The diners had quiet conversations with one another about art and literature, while they poured almond milk into their coffees and teas. The maître d' bustled about from table to table, asking the happy customers about their health and their satisfaction with their meal. He received not one single complaint, but still he could not help but cast a guilty glance toward table seven. The peace and tranquility on this side of the partition could not entirely block out the horrors occurring on the other.

Amid the gentle tones of the violin quartet and the soft clink of cutlery, customers heard hints of the battle

of life and death that was being waged in the heart of their restaurant. First a clatter of falling plates followed by an "Ouch, careful!" from Joey. Then a curse from Pierre and a thumping sound as he punched his own leg. "Pierre!! You ar zo stupeed!" Joey calmed him with "It's okay, now at least it'll match my other pant leg!"

Johnny's voice floated out: "Um, waiter, there seems to be a fly in my salad . . . oh, wait! Nope, it's gone. . . ."

Without realizing it, every soul in the restaurant was holding their breath and listening. Even the violins had stopped. The tension was so deep it spread out of the restaurant and onto the surrounding streets. No one actually said the words out loud, but the message

was clear: Joey and Johnny had made it to the entrée.

Each clatter from behind the partition made the customers jump. A roar and the sound of a large tail flapping made the maître d' drop the carafe of coffee he'd been carrying.

"Wow! That *is* surprisingly fresh!" came the voice of Johnny.

"Zirs, I forgot to offer you ze soup." There was a tremendous clang and a splash. Soup seeped from underneath the partition, eating a hole into the floor. "Mon dieu! Zo stupeed!" Soup continued to pour into the hole, as the sound of sizzling concrete came up from the basement.

"It's okay," came the voice of Joey, "it seemed a little overspiced for my taste."

Pierre ran back to the kitchen, and when he reemerged he was carrying three huge skewers dripping with meat and fire. "Come on, Pierre," he was saying to himself, "you must get thees food to zirs while eet ees still 'ot."

A woman at a table nearby mumbled, "He shouldn't be running with those," and fainted.

"Mon dieu!" cried Pierre as his foot connected with a pot of soup on the floor. There was a crash, some sharp thunks, a "Careful, Joey!" and then a "Got it, Johnny!" and finally a soft glow from shooting flames. "Pierre, what are you theenking?"

Silence followed, broken only by the crackling of flames and a dripping sound. No one breathed in the restaurant, no one talked on the streets outside. The maître d' reached for the phone to call the paramedics, and then . . .

"Do zirs still 'ave room for dessert?"

Joey walked out from behind the partition, brushing bits of burning wood and shattered ceiling tile from his ninja suit. Both pant legs were now held closed with ninja stars. "You know what, Pierre? I think I'm skipping dessert."

"Not me," said Johnny, blowing out a small fire on his arm. "I'll have mine to go."

The restaurant erupted into applause. Joey and Johnny made their way to the door, pausing to each receive a kiss on both cheeks from the joyously grinning maître d'. "You 'ave made me zo 'appy!"

Joey had his hand on the door when he gasped. "Oh! I forgot to leave a tip." He walked back to the maître d' and said, "That guy should get a job in the lunchroom at KFA, he's really good." And with that, Joey and Johnny left Snooty'Garbeux's Food'splosion and Eatery to the sound of applause and cheers. Pierre waved to them from the doorway, a tear running down his cheek. His customers had survived and that would have made his father proud.

BRAINBEAK
GOES POSTAL

In which arguments could be made
for bringing back the Pony Express.

BrainBeak burst through one of the windows of
Sensei Ohm's meditation class and chaos ensued.
She stood on the sill, eyed Joey with one of her milky-
white orbs, and then leapt toward him. Her great wings
beat the air and various students as she scrambled to
stay aloft in the confining room.

Realizing that he didn't have the hawker's glove on
him, Joey ran. The mere thought of a powdered wrist
had caused him to lose sleep.

Joey flipped backward and dove under the nearest
table half a second before BrainBeak's talons splintered
his chair back. He crawled between legs and under

butts until
he finally col-
lided with one
of Ohm's heavy
cabinets at the front of the
classroom.

Half the class mistook
BrainBeak for Sensei Kendu
and thought that meditation
and fight classes were having some
kind of bizarre crossover event. The
other half thought a small but very
fierce red-and-black tornado had just blown into the
classroom . . . and it hated Joey for some reason. Only
Spratt remained sitting still in the front of the room.

Ohm had been lecturing the class about fasting,
and how people in many cultures willingly refuse food
and water to aid in spiritual pursuits and vision quests.
To better understand the topic Spratt had decided to
skip lunch. As his belly gurgled, Spratt ignored the
calamity around him, the dark shape that crawled past
his knees, and the single blood-red feather that fell to
his desk. When the sinister hawk landed on the cabinet
above Joey's prone body, Spratt assumed that he was
having a vision. Backlit by the ever-luminous Sensei

173

Ohm, the bird slowly spread her wings and hissed.

"I hear you," Spratt whispered.

It was at this point that Sensei Ohm enveloped the bird's head inside her glowing sphere. Ohm had long ago reached such an enlightened state that she had little need for her body, existing instead as a ball of pure psychic energy. A few moments later the bird was calm. The same could not be said for the students.

"A thunderbird has brought us a message from beyond!" Spratt shouted, pointing at the feathery lightning bolt on the bird's chest.

"No," Johnny said. "That's just our bird, she—oh, wait, she does have a message."

Indeed she did. Clutched in one dark talon was a torn and dirty piece of paper. It was a letter from Ting.

Great hero is gone
Determined, I walk alone
Know I cannot fail

Okay, I seriously have to change the subject matter for my daily haikus. They've all been about Brad for the last week! Man, if anyone ever read this it'd sound like I was writing him love letters. I am

NOT, *of course. I am searching for him out of a manly sense of brotherhood and a debt owed . . . not because he's handsome. Not that Brad isn't handsome—he is. In fact, he's probably the best-looking guy I know. . . . Great, now I'm writing love letters again. Kiss, kiss.*

Know what I DO love? My hat. It totally helped with the rain, and now that things are drying up it's an awesome sun visor. I think I'm heading west. In either case, I'm moving out of the mountains. The land is really sunny and kind of flat, and there are these rock pillars in the distance. I'm going to head toward them 'cause they look cool.

Found an abandoned gas station today. Can't figure out when it closed but the sign out front says gas is 88 cents. In the back I found a vending machine. It was broken and every-thing was gone except for an entire row of Sugar-Blasted

Limon-Funberry Sponge Buns with real "frute" filling. SCORE! I love these things and supplies were getting kinda low. Lots of animal tracks but none of them touched these. Their loss.

In other news, it was nice to use an actual toilet again.

I'm going to camp at the station tonight. Wonder if I'll have that weird dream about Peoni again. Her hair's so spiky. Anyway . . .

TING

king of snacks

Johnny read the note, and read it again. Then he passed it over to Joey.

"What do you think that means?" Joey asked.

"It means someone's a *good* bird. Oh, *yes* you are. Yes you *are!*"

BrainBeak was snapping air with her beak a fraction of a second after Johnny pulled his fingers out of the way. Her feathers got ruffled, her belly scratched. All the while Johnny somehow kept his most vital parts away from the bird's beak and talons. Gradually the snaps and hisses sounded less hateful. Not exactly playful, mind you. They were still full of paint-peeling overtones, but there was something accepting at their core.

"Wow, maybe—" Joey started. At the sound of his voice, BrainBeak's milky eyes locked onto his, promising that things would go very differently for him if he ever tried so much as a scratch under the chin.

Johnny never stopped cooing. He rubbed his nose

back and forth in her black-and-red feathers. "Good, Brainy! Good girl!"

Joey held up his hands in surrender. Looking down, he noticed that the letter they wrote to Ting was still attached to BrainBeak's leg. "Yeah, goooooood bird," he whispered.

DANCING WITH WOO

In which the art of dance
loses all dignity.

Miss Woo wouldn't accept them into her class. Perhaps next year. When Joey insisted, Miss Woo asked in polite, clipped tones, "So there is some pretty girl in my class that you think you can score points with by knowing how to perform a nice jeté?" When they indicated that that was *not* the case, she continued, "No? You don't think my girls are pretty?"

"Girls!" Miss Woo yelled to a line of students performing stretches near a large mirror. "These two— What are your names? Joey and Johnny? Joey and Johnny do not think you are pretty." She turned back to the boys. "Now please go away." Behind Miss Woo the girls threw so many mental daggers at Joey and

Johnny it was a wonder they weren't pinned to the wall.

"But Wiseman told Peoni to tell us we had to," Johnny pleaded.

WISEMAN NOTE:
No, I didn't.

"Oh," Miss Woo said. "In that case, you can't join my class." The door was shut before they could say another word.

The next day the boys figured it would be best to simply demonstrate their abilities. A lot of their katas and kicks would translate well into the world of dance. The boys spent all night practicing a brief number that Johnny composed.

"She'll have to accept us when she sees how good we already are," Joey said, moving his feet with machine precision, "but I question the tap routine in the middle. We wear socks."

"*Ninja* tap is supposed to be silent," Johnny said. "Bigger smile, more jazz hands."

"I'm wearing a mask, and if I jazz hands any harder I'm going to shake my fingers off."

"More jazz hands! And we have to die at the end. Dance is supposed to be tragic."

When Miss Woo opened the door, she did not expect

an impromptu dance number, and she would later argue that she didn't get one. There were, admittedly, problems with the performance. Joey and Johnny had rehearsed in a much larger space, so many improvisations had to be made to accommodate the narrow hallway outside the dance room. They didn't bring any music, which *might* have been fine. After all, they had their own personal soundtracks playing in their heads. Unfortunately they were on completely different channels. Joey was going for something classical, but since he didn't listen to a lot of classical music it was a rough interpretation at best. Johnny was listening to classic rock.

To make matters worse the entire class, exclusively girls, gathered behind Miss Woo to watch with silent disdain. "Dance often tells a story," Miss Woo told them. "Let us see what they are telling us." Miss Woo began narrating the story of the boys' dance. The transcript went something like this:

"Oh no, the floor is lava so I must jump. Aah, more lava. Hot, hot, hot. Why did we go to this volcano? All this jumping has made me dizzy. Me too, I am so dizzy I probably didn't mean to kick you in the face. What, is that an earthquake? Maybe jumping on the lava has made the volcano angry. Everything is shifting and it has brought out the ants. Quick, quick, stomp all of the ants. Stomp them. Stomp and wave to your friend who is very far away. He does not see you. What is he, blind?

Keep waving! All the ants are dead except one, and he is very angry. Run, run from the ant, but he is very small so you only need to run in tiny circles. And keep waving, that friend is sure to see you eventually. Wait, is he ignoring you on purpose? How rude. Oh, scene change—there is a noble zebra running across the Serengeti. A noble zebra with a limp, apparently. It tries to cross the river safely, but there is a crocodile. It lunges and bites, pulling the stripy beast down into the mud. It is dying. Dying. Dead."

The flowers they had been hoping for were never tossed. The door clicked shut and there was the muffled tittering of girls. Joey turned to Johnny as they lay panting and "dead" at the end of their performance. "Well," he said, "it certainly was tragic."

Taking dance would be terrible, but *not* being allowed to take dance was intolerable. While Johnny continued to work on giving their routine a snappier opening, Joey spent the rest of the day thinking up other ways to get into class. Each idea was demonstrably worse than the one before it. When the morning came Joey gave up and decided to simply beg. Beg to be let into dance class.

He never got the chance. The door, with which he was becoming all too familiar, opened before he could knock. Zato stood there smiling at them. Being blind, he didn't look directly at them, but his smile still did.

"I hear you're taking dance class," Zato said. "Wonderful that you're expanding your horizons."

"But Miss Woo—" Johnny started.

"—has changed her mind," Zato said. Behind him Miss Woo tucked her long-fingered hands inside her robe and bowed, as if to say that there would be no hard feelings.

As the newest students, Joey and Johnny were briefly sat down while their other classmates picked up activities from the day before. Miss Woo gave the boys a quick orientation.

"Dance is beautiful, but that is not important or open to debate." She paused almost long enough to allow a question and then continued as if she hadn't. "Learning to dance is ugly. There are many things to do. When I say so, you must do them. Then you must do them again until you get them right. And again until I tell you that you got them right."

"Then we'll be dancing?" Johnny asked.

"No." She was almost offended. "I told you. Dance is beautiful. You will still be ugly."

"But—"

"If you buy a pig a shiny silver bracelet does that make it pretty? No. What about matching shoes? A sequined dress? No. That pig will not be pretty until it learns how to dance . . . and then it will be beautiful." Miss Woo glowed at the thought of it.

Joey and Johnny were directed to fetch their ceremonial uniforms from a large, dark wooden cabinet that had been rubbed with a low-luster wax. Plain, but solid and important. It was the kind of a cabinet that would hold a master's prized katana. Or the helmet of a fallen foe, perhaps with the skull still inside it.

"It's going to be tutus, isn't it?" asked Johnny.

Joey opened the sturdy-feeling doors. "It's tutus," he confirmed.

ROOM 304

In which ~~we learn important secrets~~
~~about life, the universe, and everything.~~

"Is it just me, or is Peoni not around as much as she should be?" Johnny asked. A crowd had gathered outside their stealth class. Standing at the back, neither boy could see what the holdup was. At least it gave them time to talk.

Since the boys had gotten back from Lemming Falls, Peoni had been a lot harder to find than usual. She was definitely missing classes. But she was so well known as the school's stealth champion that most teachers gave her the benefit of the doubt. Even when she *was* back, she carried a certain smugness about her. As if she was always about to sing, *"I know something you don't know."*

Joey quickly looked around the hallway just in case she was standing in plain sight. With Peoni, you never knew. "Maybe," he said, "maybe she's just working on some solo stealth project. I think she mentioned that she was practicing for her translucent belt. Or at least that's what a voice from under McJones's desk told me. It sounded like Peoni."

"I heard to get your clear belt, you have to go somewhere and put on a public spectacle without anyone seeing you."

"Just have to find an apathetic crowd, I guess," said Joey.

"When I go for it I'm going to try juggling. No one wants to see a juggler."

Vizante the Overlooked, one of the greatest stealth masters the ninja world has ever known, achieved near-invisibility by constantly asking, "Does this look infected to you?" and pointing to his butt. In eight years he was seen only once, by a bone-weary doctor who told him that it looked okay and that a warm compress would help with the swelling.

Johnny said, "I think it's something else. Like Renbow says, 'Even when the tortoise hides, his shell can still be seen.'"

WISEMAN NOTE: There was once a species of turtle for whom this was not true. For reasons

185

known only to itself—and, really, who knows the mind of a reptile?—it didn't stop after pulling inside its shell. It continued to pull and pull, until it yanked itself right out of this plane of existence. They were called popping turtles for the noise the air made as it rushed in to fill their void. They're gone now. Some say they died out. That whatever waited on the other side liked the taste of turtle meat. But who knows? Perhaps while collapsing inward they fell into some microverse where they gently swam the starways, planet-size behemoths with their own stories to tell.

Joey had had enough waiting and pushed through the milling crowd to see what the holdup was. When he reached the front of the pack he saw what they saw: a plain piece of paper tacked to the locked classroom door that read, "For the remainder of the year, stealth class has been moved to room 304."

"So what's everybody waiting for? Let's go!" Johnny said. He liked stealth class—it was like a game of hide-and-seek that you got graded on.

"Nobody's really sure where it is," said a thick-shouldered ninja named Jo Jo.

Luckily, Mai-Fan had been mapping the school to better catalog its hiding spaces. She even invented a wonderful system that cross-referenced degree of

For the remainder of the year, Stealth class has been moved to room 304.

obscurity with ease of access. Normally a pleasant girl, her face had soured. Sitting surrounded by various scrolls, Mai-Fan vigorously combed through them all and got nowhere.

Most of the rooms at KFA were unlabeled. Everyone just *knew* where places like fight class or FangSwan's office were. These were basic survival skills. When rooms were labeled it was generally using a letter/number combo: A1, D9, B4, etc. There didn't seem to be a room 304 anywhere on campus.

"This is so great!" Johnny blurted. He was talking to himself, but still managed to draw everyone's attention. Taking an unconscious cue from some of their teachers, a few students were rubbing their foreheads in expectation of what Johnny was about to say.

"Don't you see? They *hid* stealth class!"

Joey's mouth was the first to creep into a smile, but not the last. A minute later the hallway was empty as the students scoured the mountaintop, looking for their class.

LUNCH BREAK

In which we settle down
to enjoy a nice meal
in our face.

Joey and Johnny sat together in the lunchroom, picking various tidbits out of the swirling storm of food that threatened to engulf them from all sides.

"Joey! Shish kabob to your right!" said Johnny.

Joey moved his head to the left, allowing the flaming meat skewer to pass right by. "Thanks, Johnny! Reuben sandwich at two o'clock!"

Johnny snagged the sandwich with one hand and devoured it in three quick bites, "Ugh! Not enough sauerkraut. I'm gonna talk to the lunch ladies."

Johnny made it three steps before Joey pulled him back. "No! They take pride in their work. You ask and

they'll start putting sauerkraut in everything, including the doughnuts!"

The lunch ladies weren't really ladies. They were, in fact, a race of goblins who lived in caves on the KFA's mountain. They had been there for countless generations, surviving on a diet of bat and fungus. They mostly kept to themselves, but liked to throw rocks down at passersby. It was assumed that they were trying to drive people away from their homes, but this was not the case. The cave goblins just loved throwing things.

It was Zato who found a place for them as cafeteria cooks and servers, saving them from the wrath of Fang-Swan after a perfectly lobbed pebble rippled into the headmaster's tea.

They were stouter than humans, with skin ranging in color from milky-beige to a dull blue-green. It was hard to tell the males from females, but at KFA they all wore uniforms consisting of a gray and white tunic, a hairnet (only about half the goblins had hair), and a name badge that simply read "Lunch Lady." They possessed impressive upper body strength and a pitcher's aim. Ask any one of them and they'd tell you they had the greatest job in the world.

Applause burst out from the other side of the room. Joey and Johnny turned to look. Whistler had been confidently striding back to his seat with a tray piled high with sushi, tea, and chocolate cake. Totally unbeknownst to him, a handwritten sign had been taped

to his back calling the lunch ladies "a bag of donkey's noses." Judging by the size of the soup cauldron that pulverized both his lunch and dignity, that was a terrible thing to call a cave goblin.

When the boys turned back to their table, Peoni was sitting with them, eating a cup of noodles.

"Gah! Don't do that," said Joey.

"I'm not counting that one. Whistler went down hard. You wouldn't have seen me if I had been holding road flares and playing the tuba," she conceded. Then, in a much more careful tone, she asked, "So how's the Errand coming?"

"We met some superheroes; watched a great show from outer space; watched an even better show; found out Knight-Lite's a girl; met a witch and her hundred cats; Joey forgot to lift with his legs; got the tea; found a great new restaurant; and didn't get the teapot," Johnny said.

Peoni spit orange juice out of her nose. "KNIGHT-LITE'S A WHAT?" she sputtered.

"A girl," said Johnny. "They are female humans."

"*Yes*, Johnny, I *know* what girls are!" she snorted, trying to drain the orange juice from her sinuses. "How did no one know this?"

"I know!" replied Johnny. "In hindsight, boys don't usually smell like fruits of the rainforest."

Peoni shook her head. "Well, shame about the teapot; where do we stand with the unusual wood?"

"I've been looking in the library for weird wood, but it's not going . . . great," Joey said, sounding a little deflated. "'Uncommon trait'? What does that mean? That it's poisonous, or petrified? There's a story about one tree that—well, you have to put a walnut between your teeth and stick your head inside a hollow. A squirrel is supposed to come out, take the walnut, and perform a hula dance in appreciation."

Joey had to slide into Peoni to avoid being hit by a stream of mustard. One of the students behind their table had held up a naked hot dog, and the lunch ladies could not resist. The yellow-splattered student gave a wave of thanks, pulled down his mask, and started eating.

"Sounds dubious," she said.

"I know. I'd say that's more of an unusual trait for the squirrel than anything else. There's also an Asbestos Yulewood that cannot be burned. It's a pretty weird trait for wood, but it completely defeats our purpose."

"Girl-Knight-Lite and me are trying to find every body of water or mountain with the word 'blue' in it. There's like a million of them. So Girl-Knight-Lite is—"

"Please stop calling her that, Johnny."

"It's the only way I'll get used to it! Anyway, she's looking up their elevations right now. Highest wins. As a fallback she suggested I 'think outside the box.'"

"I'm pretty sure you've never even seen the box, Johnny," said Joey.

"Thanks. So far I got: Blue equals sad. Sad equals tears. You cry tears when someone dies. When you die you become a spirit. The spirits want the tea. Maybe you need to think about dead people and cry while making the tea."

"Ah, so helpful," said Peoni.

Joey leaned toward Peoni. "What about you?"

"I'm doing fine." She smiled. "Practicing." It had been so much more than "fine." Peoni had regularly been sneaking off into the woods to meet up with her pirate friends. They had been amazingly helpful. She hadn't really imagined pirates as tea drinkers, but Captain Loon said that they'd be honored. True to his word, he set up a proper tea party with real people. They were pirates instead of ninjas, but it was such a step up from practicing with bunnies and bears.

Loon had proved to be a most patient and pleasant host. Sensing her desire to keep their friendship a secret, he had not pushed to be introduced to any other ninja. And his generosity! Anytime she needed something for the ceremony all she needed to do was ask and it would be waiting for her on her next visit. This included everything from sugar cubes to a full suit of ninja tea armor. It looked just like the one in the Museum of Dangerous Things in Lemming Falls. "Ha," she chuckled to herself, "one of a kind, indeed."

He had been so helpful that she was tempted to ask him about the ingredients for the tea.

"I said, *Do you need any help?*" Joey repeated much louder than the first time.

"Oh, no. I'm okay. Uh . . . looks like lunch is over. Let's get going." The lunch ladies were herding the students toward the exits, pelting them with mints.

"Ow," Peoni said. There were so many candies whizzing through the air that it didn't really matter how fast you were. Johnny had tried to catch one in his mouth. He was left coughing and sputtering and trying to decide if he could digest a candy wrapper. There was a constant *ting, ting, ting* as Joey deflected as many as he could with his katana.

"That reminds me," Peoni said. "How is Ting?"

The brief, guilty glance Joey and Johnny gave each other spoke volumes.

The sky watches me
Waiting for a sudden shriek
Talons on my neck

If anything happens to me let this journal bear witness. It's been two days since the attack. The road is long and straight, with no real landmarks. Those pillars were getting closer but they're still a long way off. There hasn't even been so much as a car since yesterday.

I want to stress that I am not afraid of birds. Or at least I wasn't. At first I thought it was a buzzard. There are always a few circling overhead. They make me feel less lonely, sort of like the desert's version of a welcome wagon. That day there was only one, but it looked wrong somehow.

Then I heard it. Like the sound of worn-down bus brakes. No. Evil bus brakes? I'm not sure, but I do know that evil has its own sound, because I heard it two days ago.

The horrible thing dropped out of the sky like a stone. It landed in front of me and spread its wings, blocking my path. I turned to run, but it got in front of me again. It just stood there and held out one leg, clawing the air. Like it was threatening—no, promising—to do terrible things to me. Its talons looked like those little blades Professor McJones carries (I know, which ones? He carries so many blades that his coat jingles). The little black, curved knives that sound like that Muppet. Keramit, or Karambit—doesn't matter. This monster had four of them at the end of each foot.

We stared at each other for an eternity. Then it

knocked me down and started tearing at my back. Luckily my backpack got in the way. In the scuffle my journal (this journal) got knocked to the ground. The bird leapt on it like prey, tore a page from its binding, and took to the sky.

Why was I spared? Is it lining a nest? Will it be back to feed the babies? I don't know, but journal writing saved my life. Thanks, journal.

TING

thankful not to be bird poop

Avian hawk-thing
I probably taste awful
Please leave me alone

TING

Black beak tormentor
Fiendish fowl must hate my guts
Why me? Why? Why? Why?

Passed a sign that said, "Blue Mesa National Park, 14 Miles." So that's what those rock pillars are. I knew there was a word for them. The next sign told me I was entering the BADLANDS! That cannot be good.

Made decent time today. That was due mostly to the fact that I tried to outrun that horrid bird. Note to self: don't try to outrun something that can fly! Not like I had

a lot of options. I tried to fight. Grabbed a big rock to throw at it, but it turned out to be a toad that only looked like a rock. Blasted bird snatched it out of my hands and ate it, but not before the toad had a chance to pee on me.

As it feasted I ran. And ran. Got a little tired. Sat down for a bit. Ate a Sugar-Blasted Sponge Bun. It was as I packed up to go that I saw it hopping up the road toward me! Hopping with one leg in front, making that threatening gesture with its talons. After my "success" with the "rock," I decided to throw things that I knew couldn't pee on me. No effect until I lobbed my journal at it. Missed. Incredibly, the bird tore out another page and flew off. Whew. Maybe it is building a nest.

Sorry, journal, but if it's you or me . . . it's me.

TING

the hunted

p.s. I am now pretty sure the human body isn't supposed to live exclusively on Sponge Buns.

23

PEONI AND FRIENDS

In which the Legend of the
Great Tooth is finally told.

"You were doing really well until I had to kill you," Peoni said.

Captain Loon looked aghast. "But I had my pinky extended. I've been practicing since last week." He repeatedly held up his cup in demonstration.

"It's Tuesday."

He tugged at his mustache and picked up a book, one of the many books and scrolls on the subject of tea parties that he had acquired of late. Pages flipped wildly until he found what he wanted. "Ahh . . . Tuesday. You're quite right. Of course, I could've slain you twice before."

"What? When?" Peoni's eyebrows knit together.

"When you didn't ask how many sugar cubes I wanted, and again when I blotted my upper lip. You should've offered me a new napkin. That was worth at least a poke in the eye."

"But you like your tea black, and you would've had to say no to the napkin because the guest on your left had yet to use his. I was saving you the trouble."

Cornelius threw the book over his shoulder with a laugh. "Doesn't mean you don't have to ask. You're thinking about the rules all wrong. They aren't written to benefit you or your guests. They are a test of wills to figure out who can be more 'right.' Who's King of the Stuffy Jerks. Only thing is, your Stuffy Jerk gets to cut everyone in half with a sword. In my line of work, it tends to go the other way round."

"Ninjas have a lot of rules," she said.

"Pirates hardly have any. No wonder we don't get along." His gray eyes were laughing even though he wasn't. "Still, only three deaths—that's the best so far."

With the help of Cornelius, Peoni was making astounding progress. Every day brought fewer and fewer imaginary deaths. Just two days ago she died every time the dessert forks were brought into play. Now she could breeze through the twenty-seven dessert forks and was coming close to mastering the rules of the cocktail napkins.

"I couldn't have done it without you, Captain Captain." Peoni smiled.

He gave the pointy-haired girl a weary grin. To his dismay, he found himself warming to Peoni. Liking her, even. She was smart, looking for adventure, and definitely in over her head. The story sounded very familiar to him.

After working so hard to help plan it, it seemed a shame to crash her party. Maybe he could just ask for an invite.

"I think that's enough tea for today, captains," Cornelius said. The rum fumes were getting so thick at the veterans' end of the table that he feared what would happen if someone stoked up a pipe. The veterans had only participated in the tea ceremony because it gave them an excuse to slip some rum into something. Namely their bellies. And if a little tea fell in there, too? So be it.

Cornelius threw on his coat and pushed open the door. The low-ceilinged cabin was dark, and it was surprising to find the sun still high in the sky. To Cornelius it felt like they had been practicing for days.

Outside the air was brisk, so the Captain buttoned

his coat. Made of thick, velvety fabric, it was maroon with dull brass buttons, piping, and trim. Really more of a theater curtain than a jacket. It was the kind of coat that could stop a blade—and it had on many occasions. It wasn't hard to see where it had been repaired and re-stitched many times.

But the first thing anyone noticed about the coat was its size. It was _enormous_. Its tails dragged on the ground behind Cornelius and its sleeves hung way past his hands. With a stick or two in the right location, it could've been turned into a tent big enough to sleep four.

"Nice coat," Peoni said, "but isn't it a little large for . . . um, everyone?"

"It was my mom's."

"She must've been huge!"

The captain sighed and said, "Not as big as her shadow."

"Don't worry. Sensei Renbow always says, 'No shadow is as long as _something something_, nor as _something something something_ light _something_ . . . noon,'" Peoni intoned. She paused before adding, "To tell the truth, I doodle a lot in Renbow's class."

Cornelius laughed, made up his mind, and abruptly changed the subject. "Peoni," he said, "have you ever heard of the Great Tooth?"

Peoni hadn't. Cornelius pulled up a couple of barrels to sit on and signaled over one of his crew. The man wore a button-down shirt and tie under his pirate's coat. An eye patch was pulled awkwardly across one lens of his glasses. Before becoming a pirate, he had served coffee and struggled with his poetry. Now he was the ship's scribe and self-appointed storyteller.

WISEMAN NOTE: In his short time aboard the Black Loon, Captain Ship's Scribe had introduced the crew to open mic night and French press coffee. The coffee made the terrible poetry readings only slightly more bearable.

"Arrr, Cap'n Cap'n, iffn't I may?" began Captain Ship's Scribe. "I can still remember Cap'n Lookout shoutin'. '*Starboard side!*' he yelled. I ran to the rail an' saw'd nothin', so I goes te check the *other* starboard side. Dat's when I's furst saw'd it swimmin' through the inky black. The Great Tooth!"

The words drew the attention of some of the other pirates, and a small gang gathered. The captain's mustache twitched at the memory. Soon the *squonk*ing of barrels being dragged over wood was heard as crew members made themselves comfortable. One of the larger veterans had passed out on the deck and a couple of his fellows used him as a sofa. Even Captain Lookout descended from his crow's nest to listen. He got a foot tangled in the rigging and fell, flipping upside down before jerking to a halt. After struggling a moment, he accepted his fate and continued to listen with the blood rushing to his head.

"'Twas all glowin' silv'ry like the moon! But thar was no moon. It wheel'd and turn'd and spun thru the black. Smashin' thru the hull o' our ship! Yarrrr! Captain Powder Monkey aimed and fired . . . an' also put a hole in the ship. But then the veterans took over an' led us inna mighty battle."

Captain Powder Monkey smiled with embarrassment at this part of the tale while one of his mates gave him a consoling pat on the back.

"We fired an' fired again, as the beast whirled around us, but inna end it made little difference. Our ship sank, disappearing into the black. Nev'r te be seen again." Many of the gathered captains pulled their hats off and held them to their chests. A few blew their noses.

Peoni broke the sniffly silence. "It's a nice story, but you're still here. The ship didn't sink."

"We used to have more than one ship, lass," Cornelius said.

What followed was discussion of the Great Tooth itself. Even the veterans seemed uncommonly nervous at the mention of the beast. The new officers seemed somewhat less affected, their lack of experience a shield against fear.

By description the Tooth itself didn't seem that large, but there were many theories about that. Most thought it was only part of some larger sea monster. A titanic fish, half shark, half cannon, that fired its teeth toward its prey. The ghost of some whalelike leviathan whose troubled spirit manifested as a single giant tooth.

"'Tis a tooth beast," moaned one veteran who was almost foaming at the mouth. "Tooth beast, made of teeth! Its eyes are teeth, its feet are teeth, and inside its mouth?"

"Teeth?" Peoni guessed.

"TEEEEEETTH!" A couple of his mates had to restrain him, but he continued ranting about "teeth hands" and "teeth teeth." Loon strode over and grabbed the man by the collar. This was rather difficult, seeing as the terrified veteran wasn't wearing a shirt.

"It's not *here*! We've never seen it *here*, 'ave we?" Cornelius said, a bit of pirate accent coming through in his anger. "Now straighten yourself up, Captain Swab, and go grab some bunk."

Peoni hadn't seen an outburst like that since Zato announced to the school that Headmaster FangSwan would be making surprise classroom inspections.

"You—you know," Peoni said. "You've done so much to help me, maybe I could help you in return."

"Thank you, but no," Cornelius said. "I shouldn't

have brought it up. Between you and me I doubt anything can destroy the Great Tooth."

"Don't be too sure. I have these two friends, and they can wreck pretty much anything."

"I'll keep it in mind."

Long after the ninja had climbed down the rope ladder and disappeared into the woods, Loon remained outside in the steadily cooling air. From a distance he looked a bit like a child wrapped inside his huge coat—albeit a child with a mustache. He listened as footsteps approached from behind.

"Seems like a nice girl," said Captain Boatswain. He had been training to be a psychiatrist before he felt the call of the sea, and could get a pretty good read on people if he tried. "If I may be so bold, Cap'n Captain, is the plan still on?"

Cornelius took one last look into the darkening woods and sighed. "Aye, Captain Boatswain, 'tis indeed."

24

WOOD FOR THE FIRE

In which one would wonder
why wood would wander.

"**A**dmit that you're loving this!" Johnny yelled over the roar. He waved his hands in the rushing wind, holding on with just his legs. This was a questionable decision. Joey, also not holding on, folded his arms in disgust.

"I never thought that the first time I rode a dragon it would be because it owed Brad a favor." Not only did Joey have to swallow his pride and ask *Brad* . . . it had also taken the magic out of the experience. Joey envisioned fighting the dragon to a standstill, and having to team up against something even worse, like a platoon of zombie dinosaurs. In the aftermath of battle, they'd give each other a respectful nod—secretly best friends.

This felt more like Brad had set them up on a blind date.

The worst thing was how gracious Brad had been. He acted like Joey was doing him the favor. "I don't want anyone feeling like they're in my debt," Brad said. He took Joey's hand and gave it a heartfelt shake. "Thanks for helping me even the score with the dragon king. I just couldn't think of anything to ask him for."

Still, they were flying on a *dragon*! Beneath them the reptilian body was long and snakelike, but with the diameter of a school bus. Following invisible currents of air, it twisted and turned as it flew. Its wings thrummed rhythmically. With every downbeat, the leathery skin caught the air with a *thwap* so loud you could mistake it for thunder.

"Admit it!" Johnny hollered.

"All right, *fine!*" Joey said. "This. Is. Definitely ninja!"

WISEMAN NOTE: Since most dragons are no more likely to wear a saddle than you are, riding one is very hard work. You need to grab tightly to its scales and hold on for dear life the entire trip.

If you fall, it's not like getting bucked off a horse (which is also no picnic, let me tell you). Dragons tend to fly hundreds of miles an hour, thousands of feet off the ground. They enjoy the occasional barrel roll, and—yes—they do think our kind is delicious. Don't let a dragon tell you otherwise. I'm not saying that they are all vicious wyrms of legend, capturing princesses and roasting knights in their armor like baked potatoes. I am saying that if you go on a long trip with a dragon, be certain that it packs a lunch.

Of course, the trip wouldn't have been possible without Knight-Lite. After months of frustration trying to track down the spirit water, she (*I still gotta get used to that*) needed to change gears. It's not that Knight-Lite and Johnny hadn't gotten anywhere with their search. It's that they had gotten *everywhere*. Riding her hoverpony out to various *blue* lakes and springs at the top of various *blue* mountains, she collected samples in neatly labeled test tubes. Back in the Knight's armory, chemical analyzers ran a bevy of tests, but they all said the same thing—the water was just water. Like the answer to a good riddle, they'd know when they found it.

"Golly, are you sure the wiseman isn't a supervillain?" Knight-Lite asked. "About half of Night-Knight's rogues' gallery give him rhyming clues full of bad poetry."

"That would be our greatest fight ever," Johnny said. "How do you defeat someone who knows everything?"

"By punching them," Joey said. "Knowledge that you're being hit doesn't magically give you the ability to block it. That's why we train."

WISEMAN NOTE: Don't listen to him. I would make a magnificent supervillain!

Joey's research had brought him to a similar stopping point. He had walked through the shadowy catacombs of KFA's library so many times since the start of school that the librarians smiled as they shushed him. Not that Joey made a lot of noise—far from it—but that was kind of the problem. No one at KFA made a lot of noise. They were ninjas. There was no one to shush, and it had driven the librarians a bit mad. Starve one of your senses for too long and your brain will begin to struggle, wondering when it will ever use it again. A good shushing every now and then breaks up the silence and clears the head. With no actual culprit to be silenced, the librarians had just taken to shushing everyone.

On one particularly quiet afternoon Joey had faked a sneeze just to give a stressed-looking librarian a reason to shush him. She did so with gusto, then smiled as one grateful tear rolled down her cheek.

Fortunately his time there had yielded more than shushes. By comparing many sources Joey had eventually found the tree he was looking for—at least, on paper. Multiple authors, scribes, and explorers had made mention of a wood with a most "uncommon" trait. Wood that could move like an animal. Whole forests that could relocate overnight. Though it was known by many names, Joey liked Wander Wood the best.

Once he had found the wood, the trouble was . . . finding it. These trees of legend were legendary for a reason. Supposedly they had been hunted to extinction. And even if they hadn't, it seemed that no one who encountered them had ever decided to jot down a single cold, hard fact. No, they all waxed poetic about the eeriness or the beauty or the wonder without saying anything of substance. Names of kingdoms long gone were mentioned, as were rulers Joey had never heard of, so that was of no help. He could've blindly thrown a shuriken at a map and had a better chance of finding his prize.

This turned out to be wrong, because in desperation he eventually tried exactly that. After Joey removed the blindfold to see where he'd hit, he returned to the library. It's not like there was a forest in the dead center of the Pacific Ocean.

After a few more weeks of combing through book after book, Joey finally asked Knight-Lite for help. Dealing with her own dead end, the sidekick was happy to shift jobs. All the rumors and scraps of information he *had* managed to find were entered into MERLIN. Thirty seconds later its search engine produced the last known location of the Wander Wood: the kingdom of Psoapha (pronounced "sofa").

From there, Joey could piece it together. Psoapha had a mad king who hired the world's greatest hunters, woodsmen, and craftspeople to build an enormous menagerie of animate furniture that he let roam free inside the borders of his country. He did this mostly to mess with his guests and increase tourism, but it backfired. Even his subjects eventually fled to other lands for fear of being trampled by belligerent herds of tables and chairs. The kingdom fell to ruin. One day the king left the safety of his castle walls, claiming he wished to have a little lie-down on a recliner that was beckoning to him. He was never seen again. Kingless, Psoapha faded into the mists of time.

"So where is it?" asked Joey.

"Right here." Knight-Lite pressed a button on her wrist and MERLIN generated a holographic map. A red dot showed Psoapha's location. It was a little island in the dead center of the Pacific Ocean. Joey's shout of frustration was heard all the way back at KFA.

When Johnny suggested that they might need to ask Brad for help getting there, Joey's bellow could've been heard on the moon.

The dragon's neck lowered to the ground and the two ninjas eased themselves onto Psoapha's sandy shore. They were a little damp from passing through a few clouds on the way down.

"Thank you, Mr. Dragon," Johnny said.

"Although that is not my name, you are welcome, human-who-I-should-not-eat. It is an honor to help a friend of the glorious Brad."

Joey grunted in disgust. "And you'll bring us back when we're done?"

"Certainly," the dragon assured them. It gazed up and down the beach. Seeing they were alone, it added,

"Again, I wish to formally apologize for trying to roast your school."

"It's okay," Johnny said. "It was more fun fighting you than watching our whole school fall to their doom."

"Oh, good! Fire's just sort of my go-to response. I like humans," said the dragon. "I just generally like them a little crispy."

"What?"

"Uh . . . nothing." An attempt at nonchalant whistling turned a section of beach into red-hot glass.

There wasn't much left of the kingdom of Psoapha, just the ruins of a few small hamlets and the castle itself. Most of the island had returned to nature. It was midday before they encountered their first piece of feral furniture, a broad-backed love seat. Its upholstery was weathered and threadbare in places, but overall it looked healthy, sort of lived-in and comfortable. It was trundling its way out of the trees near the edge of a small clearing when the boys saw them . . .

"Babies!" Johnny cried. Three shapes tumbled out from the forest's edge. "Aren't they the cutest little footstools?" Two were upholstered just like their mother, but one had a more complicated purple fabric with dots of gold.

"Looks like dad might've had a little royal furnishing in his blood," Joey said.

At the sound of their voices, the family waddled

their way up and over a low hill, disappearing from sight. On the other side, the land dropped into a vast prairie, with herds of sofas and end tables, bookshelves and barstools. Across the landscape colors ran from blond to cherry to a low-luster walnut. Some units were fully upholstered, while others bared their naked lumber to the skies. Many had arranged themselves into little family groups, looking like perfectly coordinated living room and dining room sets spread out across the grassy fields.

The mother and her brood joined a set of similarly cushioned pieces. Two of the group's larger couches stomped to the edge and squared off against the young ninjas. When the challenge was not met they soon returned to their . . . loafing? I'm not exactly sure what furniture does.

At the edge of the plain, under the trees' growing shade, the set of tiny footstools nestled themselves against their mother's flank. Soon they appeared to be softly snoring. "Okay," said Joey, "I guess we should . . ." One of the footstools sneezed in its sleep and snuggled closer to its sibling. "Get to smashing?" Joey stood fingering the hilt of his sword, but he made no move to draw it.

"Joey, we can't turn these guys to kindling. They're too cute."

"Awww nuts!" Joey kicked the ground, disturbing a

nearby end table, which bared its drawer at him threat-eningly and then scuttled off. "Now what are we going to do? Peoni's going to think we're total failures if we don't come back with the wood!"

"Sorry, but nature's beautiful," Johnny said.

"Except when it isn't. But I agree, we can't just smash these guys. They must have a life cycle. Maybe there's a graveyard or something."

"We could find one that died of natural causes," Johnny suggested.

"Yeah."

"Maybe a coffin?"

They both stood staring at the sleeping family, confounded as to what to do next, until a commotion nearby broke their stillness. The two ninjas ran to the top of a nearby rise to see what was causing the trouble. Across the valley there was a loud clattering as frightened dressers opened and shut their drawers and writing desks smacked their tabletops up and down.

"What on earth are they panicking about?" asked Joey. He stared sharp-eyed down at the valley until the answer became apparent. Slinking among the peaceful herds like a prowling pack of hyenas was a surly gang of deck chairs. Their bodies scissored dangerously back and forth as they swarmed past quaking armchairs and terrified lamp stands. Five of them had surrounded a baby rocking chair, snapping viciously at him, while others kept the baby's desperate parents at bay.

"They're attacking the babies!" shouted Johnny.

"Shall we get ourselves some kindling?" said Joey, unsheathing his sword.

But Johnny had no answer for him; he was already running down the hill with his hammer held high over his head.

No ninja has ever, in the history of ninjas, lost a fight with lawn furniture. It was embarrassing just how close they came to being the first and second to do so. Joey and Johnny limped back to the beach much later that evening, each carrying enormous armloads of still-moving wood. Both boys were covered head to toe in bruises and a thousand nasty splinters.

"Ho there, tiny-meat-morsels-who-I-should-not-roast!" said the dragon as he uncoiled himself from the spectacular nap he'd been enjoying. "I see you are both growing spines from your skin!" he said approvingly. "It is a proud day when a young dragon grows his first spines. You will also notice scales growing in strange places and you will have funny feelings toward girl dragons!"

"They aren't spines!" groaned Joey. "They're splinters."

The dragon looked disappointed. "Sit down, soft-squishy-gummy-snacks-I-will-not-devour," he said with a sigh. "I will take care of this for you."

Both boys were too exhausted to argue, so they sat down, and the dragon, using claws as long as broomsticks and sharp as beestings, delicately removed each and every splinter.

25

FANGSWAN'S EPIPHANY

In which Fangswan tries on his colder and blacker heart.

When they arrived back at Kick Foot Academy early the next morning, one small boy named Maynard was waiting for them. He looked stricken with fear and remained that way even after the dragon made his polite good-byes and flew off.

"Maynard?" said Joey, snapping his fingers in front of the boy's glazed eyes. "Why are you waiting here?"

"Please say that you'll go to Headmaster Fang-Swan's office," the boy said through chattering teeth.

"What does he want?" asked Joey.

"He said I could live if I sent you to his office," he pleaded.

"When?"

"Yesterday," squeaked Maynard. "I don't want to die!"

"Don't worry, we'll save you," said Johnny. His voice swelled dramatically: "Let's go!" The boys left Maynard to collapse into a puddle of relief. Behind them, the boy's repeated thank-yous became the bassline for Joey and Johnny's inner soundtracks. It was the song the heroes got when they were walking to certain doom in slow motion.

The dark wood door to FangSwan's office had been recently polished. The red torchlight from the Hall of Accusation made it look slick with blood.

"What if *this* is where they moved stealth class?" Johnny whispered, and knocked with what he hoped passed for confidence.

"No one would *ever* look for it here," Joey said. It had been a long time since they lost stealth class. As of yet, no one had found room 304, but it had made "looking for stealth class" the favorite excuse for anyone caught wandering the halls.

The door opened. Stealth class wasn't inside. Fang-Swan was.

"Good afternoon, students." He was using the tone he thought sounded courteous. Joey took a deep breath, savoring the sensation of being alive.

The room was dimly lit by several candelabras. Long shadows moved and swayed as the wick and wax burned away. FangSwan was alone, sitting with his elbows on the desk, his bony fingers steepled under his nose.

"FrogPutty, PingPong—I wish you to cancel the tea party you are planning," he said.

Joey meant to respond, "What tea party, sir?" Unfortunately it came out as "GAH!"

"You can tell Zato that if he wishes to sneak about, he should not choose such noisy shoes."

The two boys stood still and silent, looking about their headmaster's office. Noticing for the first time how much furniture he had. Tall cabinets messily stacked with books, memorabilia, and taxidermied things that had crossed FangSwan loomed above them. Low benches were pushed against a wall that was filled floor to ceiling with cruel-looking weapons. A gong on long wooden legs displayed the weathered form of a dancing salamander. After their experiences on the island of Psoapha, both boys were wondering which object in the room was most likely to attack them. They silently agreed it would probably be the desk.

It was made from a section of a great tree that had been hammered into shape by FangSwan's own hands.

The curving underside had bark on it. It was battered, but it still looked like it could handle itself in a fight. In the flickering candlelight you could almost see it move.

"Is there something more interesting in the room than *me*?" asked the headmaster.

Both pairs of eyes snapped back to FangSwan. "No—no, sir," Joey said. "Sorry, sir, just noticing how much furniture you have." Realizing that this made no sense he quickly added, "We've just had a bad experience with some chairs, sir."

"Really." FangSwan twisted his head to the left, popping his neck. "All the things you must be learning at my school and we haven't taught you how to properly use a chair? I will inform the teachers to correct this."

Holding one sleeve back, he wrote with strong strokes of the brush: "Spring semester. New class. Sofa Sitting 101. Attendance mandatory. All students." He threw a handful of dust onto the wet note and folded it. Without looking, the headmaster threw the message into the air and pinned it to a wall with an iron spike. The wall was in Zato's office—in a different building.

"Now, if we have finished dancing like bears with ill-fitting vests and silly hats, tell me about the tea party."

"We're not planning a tea party, sir." Joey said. "We're just *getting* tea." This was technically true and as close to lying as Joey dared. He had never been so thankful that Peoni was the one planning and practicing in some secret location.

FangSwan stared at Joey so sharply he wondered if he was bleeding. "Yes. Of course. You needed a dragon to go to the corner store, did you? Lies and half-truths are games for children." The air seemed to darken around the headmaster. It became hard to see him, but that may have been from the blood throbbing in the boys' temples. "Are you ninjas, or children in black footy pajamas?"

At the same time Joey said, "Ninjas!" while Johnny said, "Both!"

"Like all things ninja, the tea ceremony is to be respected," FangSwan spat. "Do you even know what tea is?"

"Boiled leaf juice?" Johnny offered.

"If that is what you believe, you are already dead."

There are many kinds of bad signs. The slight quiver before an earthquake. A snake being born with two heads. The words "Falling Rock Zone" printed inside a yellow diamond. You would be wise to take heed of their warnings. I mean, who wants to be bitten by the same snake twice and then get hit by a rock? But these warnings pale next to the threat of FangSwan. At its worst a quake might cause the earth itself to rip open and swallow you whole. Horrible? Yes. But at least you knew what you were in for. There was no telling what FangSwan might do.

Over the last year Joey and Johnny had compiled a list of FangSwan's warning signs. While by no means complete, the list included: a friendly tone, a prolonged silence, laughter of any sort, being offered a choice, clapping (slow or fast), a direct interest in something related to you, and, of course, smiling.

FangSwan smiled. "New assignment: go to the gardening shed, get shovels, and dig yourselves a grave. Or two. I do not care. I recommend the east side of the mountain. Some mornings the sun rises like a burning pink and yellow egg. Quite beautiful. You can—"

"But we need to appease the spirits!" Joey inter-rupted.

"Let them be displeased!" FangSwan hissed. "The spirits are *dead*. Why should we fear them? If they were so strong, they'd still be alive." FangSwan let out a long breath, remembering tea parties past. "Like me."

Joey had just interrupted FangSwan. His entire body was tingling with fear. It felt like when you sleep on your arm wrong, only everywhere. He tried to see if Johnny was faring any better but could barely move his eyes. On his right Johnny had gone rigid. This wasn't uncommon when standing before FangSwan. What *was* unusual was the blur of motion, followed by John-ny's hammer slamming into the desk between Joey and the headmaster.

Despite having very different expressions, Fang-Swan and Joey turned as one to stare at the startled boy.

"Sorry, sir," said Johnny, putting his hammer back to wherever it came from. "I thought I saw it move."

"Sir, I—" Joey stammered as he searched in vain to find the perfect combination of words that would fix everything.

The dull flame of anger constantly burning inside FangSwan was stoked so high his skin almost glowed from within. One spidery hand made a long, slow pull down the length of his beard while his eyes kept the boys fixed in place.

"I'm afraid you will not have time to dig those graves."

A miraculously timed avian cry interrupted a scene that I would have hated having to describe for you. BrainBeak dove in through one of FangSwan's open windows with her razor talons outstretched. FangSwan made a whip-cracking gesture with his left hand that punched the air out from beneath the terrifying bird's wings, dropping her instantly to the floor. Momentum sent her rolling head over talons until she thumped against Johnny's legs. Disoriented, BrainBeak lay on her back, cawing dazedly up at Johnny.

"Nice bird," FangSwan said. "Yours?"

"Yes, Headmaster."

"It has a note on its leg. Give it to me." There were actually two notes. One from Ting and the original letter that they kept trying to send him. FangSwan's eyebrows twitched slightly as he read their contents. He folded them neatly when he was done. "Ting is gone? Looking for Brad—who is already here—and you torture him with this bird?"

"That about sums it up," Joey admitted. He realized those were most likely the last words he would speak, and they seemed very fitting.

"I have changed my mind," FangSwan announced suddenly.

"About which bit?" asked Joey, realizing he'd just made new last words and these ones weren't as good.

"You may have your tea party." He casually flipped his hand at them, and they staggered from the wind of it. "Now go."

When the executioner declares a snow day, you don't point out that it's not snowing. Neither did Joey and Johnny. They grabbed their notes and bird and bolted out the heavy door. Stopping only when safely outside, Joey turned and bowed to FangSwan. "You won't be disappointed, Headmaster!"

"We will see."

A PICNIC AMONG
THE GRAVES

In which we stop to appreciate the poetry
of the above chapter title. Ahhhhh.

The two neat graves were dug less than an armspan
from each other on the east side of the mountain. Neither Joey nor Johnny were certain that the
grave-digging assignment was still on, but it was better
to be safe than sorry.

When they had finished digging, Johnny lay down
to try out his grave. "This place is really nice. I never
imagine FangSwan liking nice things."

"Yes," Joey agreed, "the man sure knows where to
bury the bodies."

"Hey, Joey!" shouted Johnny from his grave. "I just
found the teapot!"

"What?" Joey poked his head over the side of Johnny's grave to find his friend pointing straight up at the sky.

"That cloud is totally a teapot!"

Joey looked up to see the giant floating teapot they couldn't reach. "Yeah, I guess," he said in disappointment. He lay down so he, too, could look up at the purple and orange clouds drifting overhead. The teapot had already shifted to look more like a pirate ship.

"Joey."

"Yes, Johnny?"

"If I die, you'll come visit, right?"

Joey stared at the earthen walls of his grave looming above him. "Every day."

Something silently leaned into view—a black shape against the darkening sky. Joey and Johnny could have been forgiven for crying out like bleating sheep when this happened. Their heads were full of death and tea, and they were lying in their own graves as twilight settled upon them. Ninja or no, a shadowy specter at that moment might very well incite a few high-pitched shrieks of terror.

Instead they just said, "Hi, Peoni." Peoni's pointy hair made for a very recognizable silhouette.

"Why are the two of you sitting in graves?" she asked.

Joey stood up, dusting the dirt from his uniform. "FangSwan knows about the ceremony."

Peoni said nothing, but her face grew determined. She grabbed a shovel and began digging a third hole next to theirs. Joey had to physically restrain her to get her to stop.

"No, no, no. He gave it his blessing," Joey said.

Peoni grabbed Joey by the shoulders. "He sent you to dig your own graves!"

"Ahh!" said Joey with a hint of a smile. "But he didn't actually kill us."

"Which is wonderful," came a voice from the darkening gloom, "as I am certain that your deaths would've spoiled this picnic." Vice Principal Zato walked with his customary ease across the small clearing. He had two large bamboo baskets, one in each hand.

"Vice Principal, isn't it getting a little dark for picnics?" asked Joey.

Zato set the baskets down, taking a large mat from

one of them. The blind man looked at Joey with his round black glasses. "Is it? I hadn't noticed."

He proceeded to set up several floating lanterns borrowed from Renbow's class. He lit their small candles and let them drift about the meadow like oversize fireflies. Box after box of Peoni's and the boys' favorite foods were set before them in appetizing arrangements.

"Thank you, Vice Principal. I'm sooo hungry!" Johnny murmured, staring at the feast. Other than the dried fruits and nuts the boys kept in their uniforms, Joey and Johnny hadn't eaten since leaving for Psoapha.

"Just something the lunch ladies threw together for me."

Johnny grabbed a handful of squid balls, juggling them briefly before letting them disappear down his throat. Peoni found an order of Boiled Carrot Surprise—the surprise being that it didn't have any boiled carrots. It was basically a bunch of tiny, jammy doughnuts. Joey even spied a box filled with pizza-sushi. Stretchy Italian dough wrapped around the tomato sauce and perfectly sliced tuna, held together with a single strip of dried seaweed.

Zato began setting out tea. "Peoni told me you've been quite a help. As the Ides of May is rapidly approaching, I thought it would be best to see where we stand with the ceremony."

Peoni took a deep breath and swallowed. A drifting lantern threw a spot of light on her, making her feel like she was on a game show.

Questions shot rapid-fire out of Zato's mouth, hardly leaving space for answers. "It is spring. What flower is embroidered on the napkins? The guest to your right takes two crumble cakes. Who must punish him? How? What is a Justice Cup? Four masters have been invited. Where do they sit? A core rule was broken. How do you remove the body?" And they rattled on. He never turned to Joey and Johnny for answers, which was good because they didn't know them. Thankfully, Peoni always did. Minutes passed before Zato clapped his hands in delight. "Astounding, Peoni. Such improvement! Whatever you are doing, keep it up."

Peoni quietly glowed in the praise and Johnny shot her a big thumbs-up. Zato said to the boys, "If you would, pour some tea."

Joey looked to Johnny and then back to Zato, who

gestured in front of him. Joey self-consciously picked up the pot and managed to spill only a few drops as he filled the tiny cup.

"No, no. Like Miss Woo taught you," Zato said.

"Miss Woo is our dance instructor. We never poured tea with her." Joey's voice implied that Zato might be insane. It is a tone used by many young people when confused by an adult.

"Yes, of course," Zato said. "Then dance."

The time spent in Miss Woo's class had gone more or less like the boys had expected. Every lesson was pointless and dumb and the tutus totally made their legs look fat. Sensei Woo guided them in small repetitive movements and then left them alone to practice for hours, only to come back and tell them they had done everything wrong.

While the rest of the class got to leap about gracefully like pretty fawns, Joey and Johnny had only learned bobbing and weaving motions, each of them performing a different set of moves with complicated hand and elbow gestures. They looked like a couple of broken robots unsuccessfully trying to shake hands. Joey was certain that Miss Woo was training them wrong on purpose and that the rest of the class was laughing at them behind their backs.

Zato insisted again, "Come on, now. Dance."

Joey pointed at Peoni, daring her to laugh. With

a shrug he and Johnny began shifting and twisting as they performed their dance of the deranged robot.

When they finished, Zato applauded sincerely. "Well done. Miss Woo is as fine as her reputation suggests."

"But we look like cotton-headed ninny-muffins," said Johnny.

"I wasn't going to go that far," said Joey, "but yeah, we kinda do . . ."

"Nonsense." Zato arranged a row of cups at regular intervals. When finished, he stood, holding the teapot. "Do it again."

This time as the boys began to move, Zato stepped in and placed the pot into Joey's hands, a saucer and cup into Johnny's. Their movements maneuvered pot to cup and tipped the tea inside with a perfect pour. Wide-eyed, Johnny quickly set the saucer down, and then the two of them spun to the spot where the next guest would be sitting. This time Johnny grabbed the new cup and saucer on his own.

"Joey, it's like magic!" Johnny said. Joey couldn't believe it either. Their shock should have broken their stride, but they had rehearsed the steps so many times that they continued flawlessly. Moments later five cups of tea sat on the ground without one spilled drop. Johnny whooped into the night sky with satisfaction.

"She's an excellent teacher," Zato repeated, "with fine students."

As they shared a dessert of candied pineapple slices and butter cakes, the four of them discussed the final details. Peoni produced a stack of handwritten invitations, which she gave to Zato. By this time the sky was nearly black, so the boys tried to corral a couple of lanterns closer to the blind man to help him see. The vice principal thanked them for their kindness and ignored their futility. He read each note by running his fingers over the ink. When finished he helped correct the spelling on a few of the trickier names.

"Tea and wood we have. Just the pot and water to go," Joey said when asked about the spirit tea.

Zato appeared momentarily caught off guard. "You haven't found the teapot? That's . . . surprising." He paused in thought. "Well, I'm sure it'll turn up. Sometimes the hardest things to find are right under your nose. Isn't that right, Peoni?"

"Yes, Vice Principal," Peoni mumbled.

"Focus your efforts on the water."

"Don't have to. Ting already found it for us," Johnny said proudly. "And BrainBeak ripped it out of his cold, scared hands." He turned over the note, getting a small paper cut as he did so. He sucked his finger, but was unsurprised. After all, the note *had* been folded by FangSwan.

Clear cool delicious
Evaporating away
Where did the rain go?

So thirsty! Made it to the Blue Mesa today. YAY! But I used up the last of my water. EEK! I made camp inside one of the many caves through the rock formations. Might have to try cutting open one of the cactuses I saw out— CAVE MUMMY!

Okay. There are no cave mummies. Not sure which is more embarrassing, that I thought these guys were cave mummies, or that I wrote "cave mummy" instead of running. Good survival skills, Ting.

Brother Chert is a Dust Nomad. These nomads wrap themselves from head to toe in strips of cloth to protect their skin from the blowing sand, and . . . for other reasons. I was still pretty worked up about the cave-mummy thing when he was explaining stuff and I might have missed the details.

He and his tribe live out here among the mesas. They have amazing abilities to find food and water. The food's not that big a deal. They just eat stuff that most people wouldn't—bugs

240

*and lizards and roots. The cool thing is how they get their
water. Not from cactuses, but from the sky. They say that if
the rain won't come to you, you must go to the rain. They've got
special kites and some kind of condensation/collection system.
The air's so dry that you have to fly a lot of kites, but it works.
They call it "fishing the blue."*

Things feel better than they have in weeks.

TING

cave-dwelling non-mummy

*p.s. The stones of the Blue Mesa are an orangey brown.
It got its name from the sky, not the rock. This seems dumb.
By those rules, anything could be named "Blue Whatever."
Unless you live somewhere that's really cloudy all the time.*

When Peoni and Zato had finished reading the
note, the vice principal stood very still. "Interesting,"
he said. "I had not thought of that myself, but such is
the reason you visit a wiseman."

"We still need to get it," Joey admitted. "I don't suppose a single kite holds that much water, but . . ." His
voice drifted off as he pondered rough sketches of his
ideas. They varied, but each had its own flaws, obvious
or otherwise.

They had finished off the last of the food and began
packing up their picnic. Zato neatly folded the sitting
mat as the boys chased the lanterns around, trying to
snuff them out by shouting different words at them.

Johnny used only made-up words like "clonk" and "bersnittle," while Joey tried his luck with "haberdashery" and "pudding." In case there are any members of the scientific community reading this: "clonk" puts out a lantern far more effectively than "pudding."

While the boys ran about, Peoni sat in silence wrestling with an inner dilemma. One of her secrets was clawing at the inside of her head to get out, but she knew that once she said it aloud it would no longer be her secret. So when she spoke, it was with great reluctance and a heavy sigh.

"I think I know how we can get the water."

PEONI LETS LOOSE
A SECRET

In which we firmly establish
that Peoni is not a witch.

Peoni led Joey and Johnny through the woods, following paths that only she could see. Her flitting form slid through the tree gaps with nimble ease, while Joey used his katana to cut openings in the brambles and clingy vines. Johnny simply pushed through with his hammer held in front of him like a battering ram.

"Peoni," said Joey as he briefly caught up with her, "are you actually going to clue us in on some of your deep secrets?"

"I suppose so," said Peoni, not sounding enthusiastic about the prospect. Secrets are addictive, and she'd held this one most dearly. "But you guys have to

promise not to freak out. OK?"

"I promise!" said Johnny, plowing through the underbrush. "Just don't make me promise not to break my promise. If things get hairy I don't want to break two promises."

"Uhm—" Peoni stopped in midflit. "Let's just go back to the school."

"No!" shouted Joey, pointing emphatically into the woods. "We're tired of guessing what your secret is."

"I'm not," said Johnny. "Are you an alien, Peoni? Are you taking us to the mother ship? If you're taking us to the mother ship I'm going to break my promise."

"I'm not an alien!"

"Are you a witch? Are you taking us to your chicken-leg house? I am definitely going to freak out about a giant chicken-leg house."

"I can't be a witch, Johnny. My nose is *way* too cute."

"Could be a spell, is all I'm saying."

"What is your thing with witches, anyway?" Joey asked.

Peoni carefully skirted a row of tall, dark trees that seemed to be posing like hoodlums. Behind them the wood got thick and tangled disturbingly fast. "Careful, guys." She pointed at the trees. "That's Hopalong Forest!"

"Ugh," said Joey, taking special care to keep a safe distance. "I won't make that mistake again! Last spring I spent three days stuck among those jerk trees!"

The three travelers finally broke through the forest and emerged into a wondrous glade. A shining waterfall cascaded into a crystal pool that was ringed by smooth boulders and soft green grass. The sunlight moved in

patches as the leaves shifted in the wind. Butterflies fluttered to and fro. Even against the vivid green backdrop their colors exploded like miniature fireworks.

Joey grunted in disgust. "Peoni, if you brought us here to tell us you're a fairy, *I'm* going to break Johnny's promise! I'm also probably going to puke."

"I am not a fairy!" As Peoni put a hand to her stomach, she realized there were now as many butterflies inside her as there were in the air around their heads. "It's just, uh . . . I'll just . . . introduce you, I guess . . ."

"To the butterflies? They seem to be introducing themselves," Joey said as a bright orange one landed gently on his head. "And they are not as charming as they think they are." Even more red and orange butterflies alighted upon him in spite of his frantic waving.

"Wow, Joey!" said Johnny. "If those butterflies were battle wounds, you'd look like a ferocious warrior."

"Yeah, I guess I would." Joey stood a little taller, picturing himself the sole survivor of some bloody combat.

"But they're butterflies," Johnny continued, "so you look real pretty!" Johnny easily dodged the pebble Joey threw at him.

Peoni pulled their attention back to her when she yanked on a hidden rope. This caused a ladder to drop down from the canopy of trees above them. "Wah?" said Joey as he grabbed another pebble to sling at Johnny.

"Follow me!" Peoni said as she shinnied up the ladder. She was gone in a flash, disappearing completely in the foliage above them. Joey and Johnny conferred down below.

"I don't know," said Joey. "If it wasn't Peoni leading us here, I'd think this was a trap!"

"She wouldn't lead us into a trap, Joey!" They both heard voices far above their heads. Neither boy could pick out any words, but it wasn't just Peoni talking.

"Why don't I like this?" asked Joey. But Johnny didn't answer him; he was already clambering up the ladder.

Peoni stood on the deck of the pirate ship, anxiously looking down into the trees below her. Joey and Johnny hadn't appeared yet, and now she was feeling like she should have given them a heads-up. But the words didn't come to her—the secret had been so deeply imbedded she just couldn't say it out loud.

Cornelius Loon walked up beside her, looking over the railing of his ship to see what held her attention. "Dear girl, what are you hoping to see down there?" A few members of the crew noticed their captain looking, so they too peered down.

"They're my friends," Peoni said. Suddenly she didn't know what to say to the captain either.

"You mean the two you told me about?" asked the pirate captain, frowning. "The two who keep stealing your adventures?" He gestured to three of his crew members, who drew closer.

"Did I say that?" asked Peoni.

"Why did you bring them?" Cornelius was feeling uneasy. He didn't like the unexpected. He understood

the girl. She trusted him and he . . . well, he didn't really know these friends of hers.

"It's okay!" Peoni said. Words were beginning to crowd her mouth; there were too many things she wanted to say. Too many things she thought she should have said already. "They'll like you. It's not a problem. They just want to help with the ceremony . . . like you!"

There was a rustling in the leaves below. A hand appeared, followed by a bobbing dooley-bopper. The pirate captain saw it and sucked in a gasp of recognition. Johnny's head popped into view, his eyes locking on to the captain's gaze. His gasp was just as sharp, followed immediately by an angry bellow. Johnny broke his promise and freaked out. He pulled his hammer from nowhere and ran up the remaining rungs of the ladder, screaming, "PIRATES! DIRTY TREE THIEVES!"

"What?" shouted Peoni. She could barely recognize the roaring engine of rage that was now speeding toward her new friends. "Johnny, NO! They're friends!"

The captain captain backed quickly away from the railing and shouted to his crew, "Cut the ladder, secure the girl, and cast off now!"

"Secure the what?" asked Peoni, momentarily dazed by this unexpected turn of events. The ropes that tightened around her body answered the question. Her arms pinned to her sides, she looked at Cornelius in shock and just managed to say "But—" before a sack was thrown over her head.

Johnny was almost to the top, with Joey just a few rungs behind. Joey had no idea what was going on but he knew enough to have his katana in hand. An expertly thrown ax cut the ladder inches from Johnny's reaching fingers, sending both boys plummeting into the branches below. Johnny made a desperate throw with his hammer, smashing into the ship's hull. The damage might have sunk a seagoing ship, but this was an airship. Johnny's hammer did nothing but push the boat farther into the sky.

The airship known to everyone in Badoni Dony as the *Black Loon* lifted above the trees. Its broad hull turned to the west. The huge canvas balloon above it was held to the ship by a web of thick ropes. On its weathered black surface was painted a giant skull. The ship's sails stuck out from the sides like the fins of a great fish.

An anchor, tangled with leaves and small branches,

was hurriedly being raised as it drifted away.

Falling, Joey and Johnny each caught a branch and scrambled back to the top of the tree. Johnny was nearly incoherent and Joey was still utterly confused. "What is going on?"

"PIRATES!" Johnny yelled. "They stole my family's trees—and they took Peoni!"

"They took Peoni?" Joey grabbed Johnny and pointed to a tall, slender tree. "Let's grapple that tree down!"

Together they threw hooks into the top of the tree

and pulled, bending it down until the trunk creaked and threatened to snap. They each let their ropes go and with a tremendous *thwip*, the tree whipped them high into the air.

Wind whistled past their ears as they arced over the forest on a collision course with the flying ship. Joey held his sword out like a missile. Johnny's hammer had fallen to the forest floor, but he was prepared to pound the ship apart with his bare hands. Their aim was true, but there was a flash of light that momentarily blinded them. Both boys sailed through empty space and fell back to earth in a clatter of snapping branches.

Joey and Johnny shook the leaves and dirt from their heads and looked to the sky. It was empty except for a few wispy clouds and just-emerging stars.

The ship was gone and Peoni had gone with it.

28

THE PRISONERS

In which we meet some insufferable trees
and Peoni throws the heck up.

Joey and Johnny ran through the forest, barely
feeling the sting of the sharp thorns that tried to
hold them captive. An approaching storm whipped the
trees into a frenzy. Their branches waved and shook
like the angry tentacles of a thousand enraged beasts.
A curtain of rain drew closed over the mountain,
drenching the bruised ninjas.

"We get back to the school and we tell Zato. He'll
get a rescue party going with all the teachers and Peoni
will be back in no time!" Joey shouted over the roar of
the storm, his sword swinging, cutting a path through
the grasping tangle.

Johnny swung his hammer, flattening a path for

himself. His booming hammer blows rivaled the crashing thunder that enveloped them. "Pirates!" he muttered. He'd said little else since their short battle in the treetops.

They moved a little more easily as they reached a point where the underbrush began to thin out. Fewer vines reached for them and the razor-sharp pendulum of Joey's sword strokes slowed down. "There. We're making progress. Once we hit the path we'll be back at the school."

They ran for another hour without seeing the path. There were no longer tangles or vines, only trees. The forest around them was unchanging; it didn't grow any thicker or thinner. The trees around them no longer appeared threatening—instead, they seemed . . . amused.

"Wait." Joey slowed down. "Johnny, we might be in trouble here." Johnny hefted his hammer, looking forward to having something to smash besides branches and brambles, but nothing dangerous emerged from the dark forest. There was no lumbering monster, no slavering fangs, just trees. Trees that looked very familiar, almost as if the boys had been looking at the same ones for the past hour.

"Oh no." Joey fixed his sights on a trunk that stood just three steps in front of him. He walked five steps toward it but didn't reach it. He took ten more and still couldn't touch it. Worse, it seemed to drift slightly to the right. Joey made a sudden lunge for the tree, to no avail. "Johnny, we walked into Hopalong Forest!"

Cornelius was slumped at his desk, staring at a silver flask. He turned the flask in his hand, pausing occasionally to run a finger over the name "Captain Captain Bonnie Loon" etched deeply on its side. There was a hesitant knock on the door. "Come in, Captain First Mate." Cornelius sighed, setting the flask down.

The first mate opened the door and peered around it. "Ah, Cap'n Captain, the prisoner has escaped again. I was gonna send Lumpy Joe in to check the cell."

Cornelius winced at the word "prisoner." "I told you before, Captain First Mate, she has *not* escaped. Do not send Lumpy Joe in unless the man wants another lump for his collection."

The first mate looked confused. "Er, Cap'n Captain, maybe I'm using the wrong word. Wot's the piratey word for 'no longer sittin' in her cell'?"

Cornelius's gray eyes flashed. He banged a fist on his

table and stood up. "The word you are looking for, Captain First Mate, is 'HIDING'!" He stalked to the door and pushed past the startled pirate. "I will show you!"

The brig was in the lowest and darkest section of the ship's underbelly. Cornelius pulled back the thick latch from a trapdoor set in the floor. It flopped open, revealing a narrow ladder leading down. He and the first mate carefully lowered themselves into the opening. The room below was built from heavy wooden beams bound together with solid, dark metal bolts. The prison cell was no larger than a closet, its heavy iron doors closed and secured with a padlock the size of a man's head. Its only furnishing was a small, uncomfortable-looking wooden stool, which no one was sitting on.

"Girl," said Cornelius to the empty cell, "I know you're still in there, so you might as well show yourself."

The empty cell said nothing in return, and the stool continued to not be sat on.

"I ken get Lumpy Joe . . . ," said the first mate.

Cornelius waved the man away impatiently. When the first mate disappeared up the ladder, Cornelius pulled over a matching stool and sat on it. "Come on, girl, I'm not stupid enough to open that door and you know it."

Something seemed to shift in the shadows of the cell, and when the pirate captain's eyes adjusted, he found himself looking at a perfectly visible girl with pointy hair. The look on Peoni's face was not friendly.

"They teach you well at that school of yours," he said, genuinely impressed. "I know how *we* manage to disappear, but I really can't tell how *you* do it."

Peoni said nothing, choosing instead to pummel him with her angry, accusing eyes. It was effective. Cornelius had to block the blows by looking down at his hands.

"I'm a pirate!" he said, gesturing to his enormous coat, boots, and tattoo. "Do you think I deliver balloons to children's birthday parties? Were you expecting puppies and sleepovers? *This* was the job I was born into, and I do it very well." The man's expression was so sad as he said this that Peoni nearly felt some pity for him. But then she remembered the smell of the sack as it was pulled over her head.

Cornelius tapped his boot on the floor in an effort to fill the room with something other than overwhelming silence. Peoni stayed still for so long she nearly vanished again. When she finally opened her mouth and spoke, it nearly startled the captain off his stool.

"How do you know Johnny?" she asked.

The captain fiddled with the buckles on his boots, still avoiding Peoni's eyes. "I don't know your friend Johnny, but I know his people. For a great many reasons they are not fans of me or my crew. You saw how your friend wanted to smash my ship."

"Johnny is a better judge of character than I am."

The captain stood up, slapping his hands against his knees. "Well, *he* knows that pirates don't ride around on unicorns passing out hugs."

"I didn't think that," muttered Peoni. "So what did you do to his people?" Peoni knew next to nothing about the island where Johnny was born. Her smoldering anger was getting pushed aside by curiosity.

"Badoni Dony has something that our ships need and the island residents are not keen on sharing." The captain looked down again, this time examining his fingers.

"So you've been stealing from them?"

"PIRATE!" shouted the captain, banging the heavy

lock against the bars of her cage. "I'm a blasted pirate! We don't use credit cards!" He turned away and paced the small room, straightening his mustache. When he addressed Peoni again, he spoke calmly: "We take a few trees. They have plenty to spare."

"Trees?" cried Peoni incredulously. "You're a *tree* pirate?! I think that might be worse than the unicorn-riding hug-giver!"

WISEMAN NOTE: Children, don't accept hugs from strangers who ride around on unicorns. Just pat the unicorn and move on. That goes for hippogriffs, pegasi, griffins, and wyverns . . . pretty much any fantastical beast. Double for centaurs.

"You know nothing, girl. These trees allow our ships to go where no one else can."

"What do you mean?" For the first time Peoni noticed that the light wasn't quite right. She held up her hand and looked at it. There was a faint glowing outline surrounding it, and when she waved it in front of her face, it left a vague vapor trail in the air. She looked at the captain, her eyes wide with surprise. "Wuh? Where *are* we?"

"Our ships are made of Badoni Dony Ghost Wood." He looked for some sign of understanding from Peoni, but she was clearly still confused. "Ghost Wood can disappear from the mortal realm!" He swept an arm through the air and admired the faint blue tail that followed behind. "Welcome to the astral plane, girl."

"Okay," said Joey, "I'll admit it, we may be in a bit of a pickle here." He was breathing hard and wiping sweat off his brow. They'd been running steadily for two hours, but the forest remained thick around them. Johnny sat down, and would've rested against a tree trunk, but as always they remained just out of reach.

"A pickle! I could eat about a billion pickles right now." Johnny was clutching his empty stomach. "How many days have we been here?"

"Please don't talk about food, Johnny, or how many days it's been."

"*You're* the one talking about all the pickles!" Johnny said.

The two ninjas had already tried everything in their arsenal of escape and battle techniques, but no matter how far they moved or in what direction, they still appeared to be deep in the forest. Johnny had tried smashing everything with his hammer and Joey had tried cutting everything to pieces with his katana, but the trees still stood. Never exactly moving, but never close enough to be hit, they remained untouched.

Joey had thought to mark a tree with a throwing star, but the trees seemed to curve when he threw them. He finally got a hit when he put a little backspin on the last one. A flurry of falling leaves made the tree appear to be surprised. But it didn't work. They either never saw the tree again, or it just turned so that his shuriken was always facing the other way.

Time passed wretchedly slowly. The leaves overhead obscured the passage of the sun in the day and the stars at night, but they opened wide when the rains came. The trees creaked their boughs loudly when the boys tried to sleep and dropped acorns on their heads to wake them.

"AAARGH!" Joey said. "For all we know, we might be ten feet from the edge of the forest."

"You said you were trapped here before, Joey. How did you get out last time?"

"Ugh." Joey was humiliated by the memory. "Peoni

heard me shouting and ran to get Vice Principal Zato. He pulled me out. He was really nice about it and said it could have happened to anyone." Joey winced in anguish. "I've never felt just like 'anyone' before! It must be terrible to be a normal person—they must get trapped in trees all the time!"

"Well, how did *he* get you out?"

"I don't know. He just did," Joey said. "Maybe it's because he's blind. Maybe the trees' tricks don't work on him."

Inspired, the boys tied blindfolds around their eyes, held on to each other's hands, and made a break for it. It was the first and only time either of them smacked into a tree. A nice thick trunk covered in sharp bark sent them sprawling to the ground and tasting blood.

"I guess being blind isn't the advantage I thought it would be," Joey said, taking off his blindfold and seeing no sign of the tree trunk that had clobbered them.

Johnny was vigorously rubbing the back of his head. "Don't take it too hard. Zato's blind all the time. He probably knows how to use it better."

All around them

the trees looked pleased. They probably would have given themselves a round of high fives if they'd been familiar with the gesture.

"Look, let's just try and reason with them. They must be getting bored by now."

"Joey, they're trees. I don't think they get bored."

Joey held up his hands in a placating gesture and addressed the trees. "Okay, trees? First, I want to say I'm sorry we intruded. Can you please let my friend and me go? Our pal Peoni has been kidnapped by pirates and we need to launch a rescue before they do something terrible, like feed her to sharks."

Johnny groaned. "Sharks. I could eat a billion sharks right now. . . ."

"Stop talking about eating, Johnny!"

"You're the one who brought up delicious, succulent sharks!"

The trees had nothing to say, but the cold wind blowing through their leaves sounded distinctly like giggling. All the other creatures on the mountain had long since learned to stay out of their wood. The trees had spent the last several hundred years guarding that teahouse and being entertained by gentle breezes. These little ninjas were funny. They had never imprisoned a more entertaining duo and they were not about to go back to staring at moss.

Beneath them the ninjas sat huddled in the mud.

Joey was racking his brains for new ninja-y ideas, but was too tired and hungry to think. Johnny gnawed on a handful of acorns in a desperate attempt to quiet his gurgling stomach.

Peoni was still stunned by the news that she was floating in the astral plane. She'd heard Joey and Johnny's descriptions of the place, but it hadn't made it any easier for her to accept that her body was now there. Before, she merely had to escape from a floating pirate ship. Now she had to find her way out of another world. Peoni's solo adventure was beginning to stink.

Captain Loon had hoped that his natural roguish charms would win the girl back over to his side.

"Look, girl," said the captain as he twisted his smile into what he hoped was a more charming shape. "I'm not the man my mother was. I see reason. We could work together! Let's you and I find that teahouse ourselves. We'll perform the ceremony and split whatever treasure we get!" He spread his arms in an "all is forgiven" kind of gesture.

"Who ever said anything about a treasure?" Peoni spat.

The sentence didn't make any sense to Cornelius. "No one goes through this much trouble without treasure waiting on the other side!" The girl had to be lying. He had found multiple references to a buried treasure among the books, scrolls, and papers EyeFace had provided for him.

"This isn't about treasure. It's about saving the world! If we don't do this right, there won't be anything to spend your treasure on."

"What are you talking about, girl?"

"We need to do this to . . ." Peoni didn't know how to proceed, didn't actually know the specifics. She wasn't even sure if it was the whole world that was in danger, or just the city, or just the mountain. Vice Principal Zato said it needed to be done and that was that. "The spirits, they'll, um—raise zombies or . . . uh, I'm pretty sure there's something that will explode, or shoot a giant ghost laser, or . . ."

"You don't actually know, do you?" The captain was genuinely surprised. The girl had been so self-assured.

"No! I do! It's something spirity and world-ending."

"You've spent every waking minute worrying and preparing for this ceremony of yours. Willing to risk your life. And yet you never bothered to find out why you're doing it? You're a complete trusting fool, aren't you?"

"I'm not a—!" Peoni screamed, but the last word got stuck in her throat. It seemed ridiculous to deny it from inside the cage her *trusted* pirate friend had put her in. Peoni *was* a fool. She'd trusted the pirates, Zato, and some weird naked wiseman on a mountain. She even trusted Joey and Johnny (eventually). Worst of all, she'd trusted herself. "I just wanted an adventure of my own," she said sadly, but quickly rallied. "*I thought you were my friend!*"

"I am . . . a *pirate*, girl," Cornelius said. "I thought I made that plain."

"Well, then *you're* the fool. Your mom forced you to be a pirate."

"I knew it was a mistake to tell you about my mom," he growled. "Anyway, it's a calling! She didn't force me, the sea is in my blood!"

"Yeah?" Peoni pulled her face as close to the captain's as the bars of her cell would allow. "Who told you that one?"

"My . . . uh—" The captain's answer was cut short by Peoni's self-satisfied grin. Cornelius's face darkened. "You should count yourself lucky. A little girl, locked in a cage, onboard a flying pirate ship, stuck in the astral plane. How much more adventure could you ask for?"

The trapdoor slammed behind him and Peoni was left alone with her "adventure."

"Okay, wait!" Joey smacked his own head as plan number two hundred and eight came to him. He explained it to Johnny as he knotted their climbing ropes together. "We can't walk out, so we'll have to fly."

"I tried that," Johnny said, "but I'm only good at it in my wonderful imagination."

"Aha!" Joey said. He secured one end of his extra-long rope to his ankle, the other to Johnny's wrist. "But this is different. This will work! I need you to hit me with your hammer."

"I think I know where you're going with this, Joey. I kill you with my hammer and then you fly out of here on your angel wings. Good plan, but it's got a steep downside: your harp playing is an embarrassment."

"That is *so* not the plan, Johnny. You're going to hit me out of the forest with your hammer, and then I'm going to use the rope to pull you out after me."

"Joey, I—"

"Peoni needs us, and I am not going to be felled by a tree!" An acorn dropped squarely on his head to punctuate this. Johnny agreed hesitantly.

Joey picked a direction by spinning around and pointing. "If this doesn't work, tell everyone I died fighting a ferocious beast. Something with wings and tusks and fur . . . maybe it had icy breath, or fire . . . no, make that lightning."

"I promise to make up something horrible." Johnny readied his hammer, pulling back his arms like he was preparing to hit a home run into outer space.

"Promise not to pulverize me."

"I promise never to pulverize you unless for some

267

reason you become a zombie."

"That's fair." Joey leapt and Johnny swung. The resulting *crack* echoed through the forest as Joey shot skyward, plowing through grasping branches like a cannonball.

His cry of "Soooooooooooo ninjaaaaaaaaaa!" was heard across the whole of the mountain and far down into Lemming Falls.

Peoni worked at the lock on her cage for three hours before remembering that she'd been in the forest learning to speak

chipmunk during lock-picking class. "A thousand drats!" she cursed, throwing another twisted hairpin to the ground. There was a sizable pile of them at her feet. "How can this be so hard?!"

The sound of an iron bolt being drawn pulled her attention to the trapdoor in the ceiling. She momentarily feared that it would be Joey and Johnny mounting her inevitable rescue. Peoni wasn't ready for that humiliation; Joey would almost certainly be smug about it. She breathed a sigh of relief when the first mate's head appeared. "Hey, girl, the cap'n captain wanted to know if you needed anything."

This was her chance! Peoni had done well in Miss Woo's class; she would use the power of dance to enchant the first mate into doing her bidding. First, a magnificent welcoming smile, then a slow, rhythmic batting of the eyelids to draw him in.

The first mate came down the ladder, his eyes transfixed on Peoni. It was working! Peoni closed her eyes, concentrating harder. She cleared her mind of all hostility and ugliness. Only beautiful thoughts: "I am a flower. No, a butterfly . . . um, an ocean! Of tranquility and endless loveliness." The first mate stood slack-jawed, staring. Now he was her prisoner. She concentrated even harder. "I am an endless blue sky; I am fathomless bright stars twinkling in your empty skull. . . . Boy, this would make Joey sick. . . . No, stop it! I am, uh . . . a lovely landscape with cows. . . . Joey would literally vomit if he . . . gah! Butterflies! Sweet iridescent bee wings! Stop throwing up in my brain, Joey!"

The first mate stood right in front of her cage door, holding something in his hands. Was it the keys?

It was a bucket.

"You a'right, luv? Your face went all wonky and I thought you wuz gonna throw up!"

"Throw up?" Now she was doubly glad Joey hadn't just seen her.

"Astral plane'll do that to ya, no shame innit," he said. "Much worse on deck till you get your sea legs."

"It's true. I am!" said Peoni. This place did make her feel queasy. She concentrated on everything that made her sick, piling it on top of what she already felt. FangSwan's office, screwing up the tea ceremony, pretty much everything FuShoe did. The memory of that sack being pulled over her head tipped her over the edge. Peoni lost what little she'd eaten into the bucket while the first mate held it and politely looked up at the ceiling. When she was done, she wiped her mouth and sat back on the stool with a weak grunt.

"You all done, luv?" He smiled at her. "Don't worry, Cap'n Captain says we're gonna jump to normal space soon."

Peoni nodded weakly. The first mate left a fresh bucket for her and climbed back up the ladder. He went up faster than he came down. It was probably because his key ring was just a little bit lighter.

Joey awoke with his arms wrapped tightly around a tree; his head felt mushy and the world was fuzzy. "Wah . . . wuh happnz?"

"You hit a tree, Joey," said the blur kneeling next to him.

"I hit a tree? Why don't I remember that?"

"I'm guessing it's because you hit a tree."

"Why am I hugging it if it hit me?"

"Because it's the only one that's been willing to hug you in days."

Joey carefully moved his body in an effort to find out if anything was broken or missing. The enormous pain in all his body parts told him they were still attached to him. He rubbed his eyes and Johnny came a little more into focus. "I hurt in my everything."

"Yes," said Johnny, pulling a still-smoking fish out of the fire and handing it to Joey. "I think maybe hitting people with hammers into trees isn't good for them."

Joey devoured the fish in a single ravenous bite, and Johnny nearly lost his fingers giving him a second one. "Wegotawayfromthoseblastedawfultrees!" Joey spluttered in between mouthfuls of blisteringly hot fish.

"Yes! And it only took eighteen tries!"

Joey poked in his mouth to see if all his teeth were still there. "You hit me eighteen times?"

"It was hard on me too, Joey," said Johnny, looking hurt. "My arms are aching!"

An unearthly shriek caused a flock of butterflies to scatter in fear. A dark form swooped among them, snapping viciously at their bright wings.

"Oh, and BrainBeak's back," said Johnny, gesturing to the scene of horrific carnage. BrainBeak flared her wings like a tiny vampire and turned to give Joey a look. Her beak was stuffed full of butterfly, giving her a pretty smile. "She brought more news from Ting!" He handed Joey some crushed, torn pages.

Nights shiver with fear
Sunlight offers no respite
From the wide blue sky

I am cursed. Either that bird hates me, or it's a big fan of my writing. Can it even read? Bird's generally can't, right? Long story short—it attacked again and took even more pages from this journal. At this point I'm basically writing in fear that it would get angry if it found a blank page. Bird, if you are reading this: PLEASE, JUST TELL ME WHAT YOU WANT!

It struck in the night, because it can apparently see in the dark. I awoke to the monstrous thing poking me in the face with its talons. It had found me INSIDE THE CAVE. I decided right there that if I was going to go down, then I'd go down like that rock toad . . . peeing in terror.

Brothers Arkose, Chalk, Flint, and Chert tried to help fight it off but it made surprisingly short work of them. No real injuries, but it knocked them about the cave until I finally grabbed my journal and flung it outside. The demon followed and then flew into the sky with its paper prize.

I left the nomads this morning, with my supplies gratefully replenished. They are a good people and don't deserve the evil that flies behind me. And what about Brad? If only the heavens had sent me a sign of his whereabouts instead of this foul raptor! I've been so terrified my quest has been *nearly forgotten. No more. Brad's still out there somewhere, and it's up to me to find him.*

TING

enemy of avians, finder of Brad

p.s. Did you read that last paragraph? AWESOME! Sounded like I was in a movie or something. And was the hero! I could almost hear the determined but slightly sad music swelling up behind me. I wish we had soundtracks in real life.

When Joey was done, Johnny said, "He almost seems happy."

"Should we keep sending BrainBeak to Ting? I know we're trying to tell him about Brad, but he's still hasn't gotten the message, and I'm pretty sure we're scaring years off his life."

Johnny ruffled BrainBeak's head feathers. "But

she's such a good bird! How else are we going to find him?"

"I just wish we could find Peoni as easy as . . ." Joey's mouth stopped working midsentence. He jerked his head toward the bird. She gave him an angry hiss and ate another passing butterfly. Then Joey put down the note and grabbed a blank journal page off the ground. Smoothing it out over a rock, he said, "We're gonna need a pen."

It wasn't common for Johnny to give a confused look to Joey, but he did so now. "And why would we need that?" he asked.

"Because," said Joey, "we're going to write the pirates a letter and tell them how we feel."

29

TELEGRAM!

In which another terrible thing happens involving pianos. What are the chances?

Captain Captain Cornelius Loon was pacing the deck, considering his options. The girl was lying about the treasure. And she wasn't likely to tell him what he needed to know without some leverage. He needed something she cared about.

"Ahhh, Cap'n Captain?" His first mate approached him, looking embarrassed.

"What is it, man?" the captain asked in a tone that made the first mate put his hands up in defense.

"Ahhhh . . . we sorta found Lumpy Joe wit another lump on 'is 'ead. He's bin knocked on 'is noggin wit a seasick bucket."

Cornelius bent to his knees and clapped both

hands against his forehead. He stayed that way for a few moments, leaving the first mate to awkwardly shuffle his feet while he waited for an order or a punch. When the captain stood up again he breathed out one calming breath and directed his gaze back at his terrified man. "The girl's escaped." He leaned against the ship's railing and looked down at the forest hundreds of feet below. "She has no way off this ship. Send men to find her. She'll be hiding really well."

"Ah'll send Tommy TwoNoses after her, Cap'n. He'll suss her out right quick."

"Do it, and send Four-Arms Finnegan with him. That girl's no joke."

The first mate paled and stammered, "Uh, Cap'n, Finn's readin' 'is book. I'd hate to bug 'im."

"Bug him! Captain Captain's orders!"

The first mate ran belowdecks, tripping over the stairs on trembling legs. Cornelius returned to his pacing, trying to compose his thoughts once more. A murky plan began to solidify. Before it became clear, another shout disturbed his mind like a stone into calm water. This time it was the voice of Captain Lookout. "Cap'n Captain! Off the starboard bow, we got a nasty-looking bird headin' right for us!"

The raptor landed on the lookout basket and held out a leg. There was a note clutched in its talon, which the lookout carefully took and unrolled. "Uh, it's a note, Cap'n Captain. Looks like it's been written in berry juice."

Cornelius looked up at the great balloon between him and his lookout incredulously. "I don't care what it's written in! What does the blasted note say?"

The lookout mouthed the words to himself before saying out loud, "Uh, I think it says, 'Ut OH, you poked the BUNNY!'"

The next thing that left the lookout's mouth was three of his teeth as a black-clad foot connected with his face. The teeth bounced off the balloon and clattered to the deck in the midst of the sur- prised pirate crew, just seconds before Joey and Johnny did.

Joey held his katana out in front of him with two hands while Johnny hefted his hammer high overhead. "We'll be taking our friend back now, thank you very much," said Joey.

"Nice use of manners!" said Johnny.

Cornelius pulled out his sword. The hilt was an ornately carved silver loon's head whose curving beak formed the glimmering blade. He spun it once in his hand. A cleverly positioned hole near the blade's tip made the sword sing the same mournful cry as the bird it was crafted to look like. The captain had just found the leverage he needed to convince the girl to help him. "Every man on deck!" he shouted. "Capture those boys!"

Everyone made a sound at once. The pirates shouted as they threw themselves at the two ninjas in a massive tangle of thick, strong arms and sharpened steel. Joey and Johnny roared back, unleashing days' worth of frustrated, captive worry. BrainBeak shrieked loud enough to make several pirates clutch their ears in pain before she took to the air.

"Good bird!" Johnny yelled. "Go tell Zato!"

Joey's sword cut through the grips of five hatchets and six long daggers with one vicious sweep. The pirates fell back momentarily as they dropped the remains of their weapons. Their attack resumed almost immediately as they pulled replacements from the seemingly limitless supply on ship. There were ropes and chains, metal hooks and wooden belaying pins. Everything on the deck seemed to be made for murder.

Johnny bought Joey a little breathing room by bouncing off the ship's main mast and plowing his hammer into the deck. The blow sent splintered floorboards spinning into the air and knocked five of Joey's most persistent attackers off their feet.

The chilling sound of a loon's cry warned Joey that the ship's captain had joined the fray. The sharpened beak whistled past Joey's ear as he flicked his katana up to deflect the cut. A second, third, and fourth strike followed in quick succession, giving Joey no time to launch his own assault. The loon blade was a near-invisible blur always just inches away, its sound boring deeper into Joey's head. A rapid thrust got past Joey's guard, sending his katana spinning out of his hand.

"Nuts!" cried Joey as he ducked under a kick to his head, rolled to avoid an ax, leapt to dodge an iron cudgel, and slid across a wet section of deck to retrieve his

lost sword. He pulled it from where it had stuck fast in a wooden barrel and raised it just in time to deflect another bombardment from the pirate captain's saber. Cornelius said nothing as he attacked—even if he had, it would have been impossible to hear anything over the sound of his weapon. The man's eyes showed a look of total concentration as his blows rained down tirelessly. Joey was exhausted, his body battered from days of captivity in the forest. Another flicking thrust once again separated Joey from his sword.

Woooo o o o o o o o o o o o o o o o

The veteran known as Four-Arms Finnegan didn't actually have four arms. He had the traditional number (which is two, if you're into counting). Each arm was so massive that it could easily count as four (which would give you eight arms total—pirates are not particularly good with math). When the man wanted to arm-wrestle he'd challenge the whole crew all at once and still win without even a grunt of effort. He'd acted as the ship's main enforcer when Bonnie Loon ruled over them, but to his frustration he'd found himself unleashed far less under the leadership of her son. It had given him plenty of time to read, and he'd taken particular interest in titles such as *Be Your Own Boss, You're a Man! Take CHARGE*, and *I'm Okay with Mutiny, How About You?*

Tommy TwoNoses, on the other hand, actually had two noses. They sat side by side on his face like two uncomfortable passengers forced to share the same seat. He was roughly a third of the size of Finn and had to scramble in front of the larger man just to avoid being squashed. It made Tommy look less like a person and more like an anxious, rat-faced dog being

taken for a walk. It didn't help matters that Tommy was twisting his head side to side sniffing the air from each of his four nostrils.

"She's here, Finn. I can smell her shadow."

The two were searching the depths of the ship's inner workings, passing by countless baskets piled high with reeking pirate laundry. Tommy's noses were working hard to separate the smells of laundry soap and old sweat from the nearly invisible scent of one ninja girl.

"Just point to her hiding spot and ah'll club it till it stops being her hiding spot," Finnegan said. He flexed his fingers around a chain that appeared to have a small piano hanging from it.

"Ah'm pretty sure the cap'n wants this one uncrushed, Finn."

Finnegan had been pulled away from a rather interesting chapter about the importance of taking the reins and handling problems with "your own personal style." He was feeling eager to put what he'd learned into action. "The captain is going to have to settle for a bit crushed," he said while smashing a barrel of dirty socks flat with his piano.

Tommy leaned his head back and breathed long and deep through his pair of snouts. He blinked his eyes and clucked his tongue as he sampled each fragrance. Then, with soft "Ah," he swiveled a finger to an empty spot in the room.

Finnegan's piano played a one-note concert as it whistled through the air and detonated against the seemingly empty spot. *BA-DOOOOOOOOOONG!* Peoni rolled aside amid a shower of ebony and ivory keys. She snapped quickly to her feet, suddenly very much visible. Glancing at the snarl of broken piano parts scattered around her, she said, "That seems like a waste!"

Finn gasped at her accusatory tone and in a wounded voice he said, "I don't waste 'em! In betwixt smashin' fellas with pianos, ah like to spend my time fixin' 'em up again." He pulled at the chain and began swinging the piano's still-sturdy frame in a threatening manner. It continued to tinkle musically.

"Oh, well . . . that's sort of nice." Peoni had a great respect for recycling. She couldn't help but like Finn just a tiny bit for his consideration toward the environment. She would still need to beat him up though. A gray, abused mop was leaning against the wall behind her; she snatched it and held it out in front of her like a sword. "Now I'm going to, um . . ." She knew Joey and Johnny would say something really cool right now and racked her brains to come up with something. "I'm going to hit you with this."

"Look at that, Finn," said Tommy. "She's goin' ta hit you wit' a mop! I bet she's gonna try an' mop the floor wit us!"

Peoni fumed. That was a much better quip. She was in grave danger of losing the verbal part of this fight. Maybe she could make a piano joke. "Yeah? Why don't you, um . . . make like a piano and . . . uh, tinkle?"

"Hey, Finn! I think I heard a note o' derision in her voice. Why don' you show the wee girl wot a note o' derision is supposed to sound like?"

"GAH!" thought Peoni as she ducked under Finn's attempt to play all the remaining keys on her head. "These guys have really good material."

Joey had just lost his sword again. It was getting embarrassing. This time he spotted it high up, sticking out of the main mast, right where it disappeared into the bottom of the black canvas balloon. "Johnny!" he called, pointing up at it. "I need a boost!"

What he failed to notice during his fight with the captain was that Johnny was now left fighting the rest of the crew by himself. His hammer thumped and thwacked its way through the snarling crowd, but every opening he made was just as quickly filled. Johnny gave his friend a brief nod and somersaulted over the backs of his most persistent foes, landing within a hammer's swing of Joey.

"Gently this time," Joey pleaded as he twisted aside from another swing of the wailing loon blade. Joey hit the deck, rolled under the captain's legs, and leapt toward Johnny. His friend's hammer heaved up just as Joey's feet touched it. As requested, the hit was gentle, but still easily catapulted Joey into the ship's rigging.

The captain turned the loon blade toward the boy from Badoni Dony. Johnny's dooley-bopper swung in concentration. A relentless tide of pirates threatened to wash him overboard, but they still underestimated just how hard he could hit things with that hammer. He channeled the rage and frustration of the last few days, putting it all into a two-handed swing that burst twenty feet of the ship's deck into kindling. The resulting shockwave spilled every pirate off his feet and momentarily silenced the wailing loon blade as it was sent spinning from the captain's hand.

Joey yanked his katana from the mast. From up high he caught sight of the captain scrambling for the loon sword. "Ha!" he said as he pulled a rope from the tangle above his head. He hummed an appropriate heroic tune as he swung down from the rigging to land inches away from the captain's lost sword.

WISEMAN NOTE:
If you should ever find yourself swinging from a rope aboard a pirate ship in midbattle, you will play action music in your head. Everyone does.

"So," Joey said as Cornelius stopped dead in front of him. Joey's sword was pointed at the captain's chest. "I guess the boot is on the other shoe, isn't it?" Joey reviewed what he had just said in his head. Curses, it was like something Peoni might say! Those trees took more out of him than he had thought. "Just call off your crew and give Peoni back."

The captain's crew had caught wind of what was

going on, and a momentary hush fell over the battle as everyone waited to see what Captain Captain Cornelius Loon would do. Johnny was breathing hard but still held his hammer high overhead in preparation to wreck some more deck.

Cornelius stepped closer to Joey's sword, allowing the tip to rest against his shirt button. "No," he said.

"Uh . . . ," said Joey.

"You can have the girl when I know how to get to the teahouse," continued the captain, pushing forward a little more. The sword cut his button in half. Joey watched the pieces fall to the ground between them. This rescue wasn't going at all to plan.

"Cut him in half, Joey!" yelled Johnny. Wow. Johnny really didn't like pirates.

Joey ignored Johnny's well-meaning advice. Instead he said, "We don't know where the teahouse is."

"Then convince the girl to tell me."

"We can't even convince the girl to tell *us*!" yelled Joey. And that's when he was nearly smacked by a piano.

The piano had smashed through the lower decks with a force that would've made Johnny's hammer jealous. It also seemed to be attempting to play "Flight of the Bumblebee" as it passed within millimeters of Joey's face. Cornelius ignored the piano and leapt straight for the loon sword. In a smooth roll he recovered it and flipped back to his feet to face Joey.

Joey didn't even notice. He was distracted by the guy swinging the piano and the sudden reappearance of Peoni. "Peoni!" he shouted. "YAY! We rescued you!"

Peoni jumped over the spinning piano and gave Finnegan's head another whack with her mop. She landed near Joey, shouting, "No! This doesn't count. I got myself out!"

"Don't you belittle our rescue!" shouted Joey as they both jumped over the piano again. "Poor Johnny is fighting the entire crew for you!"

Peoni glanced over at Johnny, who took a brief moment in between boat-shuddering thumps to wave to Peoni. "Yay, Peoni! We rescued you!"

Peoni flipped and wove over the crew so she could get close enough to explain to Johnny how he didn't rescue her. Joey heard the call of the dreaded loon sword again and parried its silver beak as it streaked toward his head. In desperation, he managed to put the man with the spinning piano between him and the captain and landed near to where Peoni and Johnny were arguing.

". . . and that's why you"—Peoni paused to bash a pirate with her mop—"did *not*"—she tripped another, who fell down and was immediately trod on by three of his mates—"rescue me!"

"So you had"—Johnny swatted five pirates, who clattered to the deck in an explosion of loose teeth and eye patches—"a plan"—he jumped back to avoid a clumsily thrown net—"for getting off the ship . . . ?"

"Uhhh . . . yeah!" She took her time beating up the pirate who was flailing a trident at her. She needed a minute to think. "I was . . . gonna make a parachute!"

"What? Did ya bring yer own sewing machine?" asked the man with the trident.

"Grrrr!" Peoni knocked out the man with the trident.

"Soooo . . ." Johnny gestured to the pirate's unconscious body. "Are you going to answer the man's question?"

"How were you and Joey going to get off the ship?"

"We brought hang gliders!" Joey said.

Cornelius watched the three ninjas huddle together, linking arms while Johnny continued to use his hammer to keep the pirate horde at bay. "Finnegan!" yelled the captain. "Flatten them!"

Finnegan smiled. Even the captain captain's mom had rarely given Finnegan a command with so much destructive freedom. He snapped the chain and happily hurled the piano with the force of a cannon. Airborne, its remaining keys nearly banged out "Ride of the Valkyries." Peoni saw it coming, but they were boxed in. The jangling instrument of doom was going to crush pirate and ninja alike.

Johnny swung to face it. The clown hammer met the piano head-on and pulverized it with one final thunderous chord. The force sent pirates sprawling and knocked the ninjas to the ground. Bits and pieces rained down upon the ship, sounding like a hurriedly disbanding orchestra. It was only after the last ivory key fell that any of them began to stir.

From the bow, Cornelius Loon bellowed, "All hands, prepare to phase ship!"

Next to the large wooden wheel, a lever was thrown and the world went black. Air rushed in to fill the empty space as the ship, its crew, and three battle-weary ninjas were pulled out of this world and into another.

Cornelius was ready to congratulate himself; he'd proved himself master of the ship, and now the ninjas were effectively his prisoners. They had nowhere to run. And if that piano hadn't taken the fight out of them, it didn't matter. His crew had their sea legs and the ninjas didn't. The fight would go very differently this time.

But his crew wasn't making sounds of victory. A scream went up, a horrified shriek of fear. There was panicked running and men were leaping over the side. What could possibly cause such a . . . The captain stopped—his sword dropped from his hand.

The boy. The tall one from Badoni Dony. He no longer held a hammer. The object in his hands blazed a bright silvery white and roared silently.

The boy held the GREAT TOOTH!

30

THE GREAT TOOTH

*In which we find out
that the Great Tooth
was Mr. Wickles all along!*

"**J**ohnny? What's going on?" Peoni stared at the glowing hammer. Joey was looking at the empty deck.

The pirates were gone. They jumped overboard rather than face the terror of the Great Tooth. It seems like an odd decision, but you need to see it from their perspective. Imagine that there's a great white shark that bit off your leg. You spend years living in terror that it might come back for the rest of you. At the same time you're obsessed, desperately trying to discover a way to destroy it. You also like tennis. One day in the middle of a match your opponent unexpectedly switches rackets. His new racket is that great white shark.

You might have gone mad, too.

Cornelius was the last of the pirates to go. Pausing only long enough to grab his mother's enormous coat before giving one final, disbelieving gaze, he dropped over the side.

Joey stood and sheathed his katana. "If you told me I was going to sustain multiple piano-related injuries this year, I would've called you a liar."

"Weird, huh?" Johnny mumbled, entranced by his glowing hammer. He swished it around, forming a bright figure eight that blazed for a few moments before fading back into the dark.

"Why is your hammer glowing?" Peoni asked, her voice sounding muffled in the astral air.

"I have absolutely no idea. My parents told me the hammer was special when they gave it to me, but then they said the same thing about every crayon drawing and mushy animal sculpture I made, too."

"I think they were right about the hammer," said Joey. He reached up to brush his hand through the hammer's vapor trail. It was warm and left his hand tingling.

Johnny gave his hammer a fond pat. "Who's a good boy? Who's a good dirty, stinking, tree-plundering-pirate pounder?"

"Why do you keep mentioning tree plundering, Johnny?" Joey snapped his fingers, trying to pull Johnny's attention away from his beloved weapon. "What trees are you talking about?"

"The Ghost Wood trees!" answered Johnny. "My family's island is sometimes covered in Ghost Wood trees."

"What do you mean by 'sometimes covered'?"

"It's Ghost Wood," said Johnny, as if that were enough explanation. When he noticed his friends' confused expressions, he added, "Ghost Wood trees go away when they want to."

"The pirates mentioned Ghost Wood!" shouted Peoni, smacking her fist. "Cornelius said his ship was made of the stuff." She put her hands on the ship's railing and looked out into the fathomless dark. Far on the horizon she could see pinpricks of light and larger glowing forms that could have been distant islands. "I think we know where your trees go when they feel like leaving!"

"And let me guess," said Joey. "Your hammer is made of Ghost Wood, isn't it?"

"According to my dad, my hammer is made from the heart of the matriarch of the whole forest. The tree was struck by lightning before I left for KFA, and he had it made into a hammer for me."

Joey stomped the deck in anger. "You have an enchanted weapon made from lightning and mumbo-jumbo and you didn't tell me?"

"I didn't know it was a magical weapon!" cried Johnny. "Dad and I used to play croquet. I just figured it was a fancy mallet." He spun the hammer in his hands while all three of them gazed at it with new-found respect.

"Well, no wonder it hunts pirates," said Peoni. "They've been stealing your trees and your hammer has it in for them."

"Well, I'm still not calling him the 'Great Tooth,'" said Johnny. "That's a dumb name. I'm calling him 'King Crunchy' today!"

Peoni clutched at her stomach and gripped the railing tighter to keep from falling. "I don't feel great, guys—can we go back to the real world?"

"We were just hit by a piano," said Joey. "We're allowed to feel bad. Johnny, how are you holding up?" Johnny didn't respond. He was too busy writing his name with the silver trail of his hammer. The sight made Joey suddenly feel a little dizzy. He burped and put a hand to his stomach as well. "Okay, I'm taking us back." He threw the lever and the world bloomed into sunlight and blue sky.

When they dropped anchor at KFA hours later,

Zato was waiting for them. BrainBeak had delivered the message:

"I don't know why I let you write the letters," sighed Joey.

"What?" Johnny seemed taken aback.

"Well, for starters, he might've thought *we* were pirates. Seeing how we sailed here in a *flying pirate ship*."

Peoni spoke to Zato: "For the record, I saved myself," she said. Which got two snorts of disagreement from the boys.

"I'm sure you all honored the teachings of Fang-Swan. I would expect no less," Zato said. "What of the water?"

"What water?"

Zato cleared his throat. "The *spirit* water that you left to retrieve."

"Oh . . . sorry, Sensei," Joey said. "Kind of a lot

happened since we left."

"I'm the Great Tooth!" Johnny offered.

The water, thankfully, was no problem. When Peoni read Ting's letter, she already knew from her time among the pirates that they gathered their water in much the same fashion as the desert nomads. Hundreds of gallons were already on board.

Having their own pirate ship solved another problem that they didn't even know they had: transport. The ceremony was going to require a lot of supplies, and they no longer had to worry about how to get them to the teahouse. Even better, the *Black Loon* was loaded with stuff Cornelius had acquired for their practice parties. Having a captured flying pirate ship was turning out to be the best thing ever.

Even FangSwan visited once as the boys were loading more glassware onto the ship. He stopped next to the anchor and looked up at the hovering vessel. "Bloodthirsty pirates or comedy-singing pirates?" he said.

"Bloodthirsty, sir!" they said in unison. To which their headmaster frowned a little and returned to his office, but not in a dismissive way. Joey and Johnny told the story of it for days, never failing to get an impressed reaction from their listeners.

Peoni also had a surprise; someone had made dessert: cakes and crepes, sweet buns, cupcakes, and tarts. There was a huge tray with cookies shaped like throwing stars and ninjas. Some of the ninjas had hammers, and a few even had spiky hair. The pastries rested on tables ready to be loaded.

"I-I don't know what to say," Peoni said. As with everything else, the food for the ceremony followed  exacting rules, which were punishable by death if violated. In her training Peoni had learned the recipes but had not yet had time to bake them.

"I am certain 'thank you' will suffice." Zato smiled and stepped aside.

Behind him stood three of the lunch ladies, who looked awkward outside of their kitchen. They had prepared it all. But the amazing part was none of it was flying through the air. Each delicacy was in its own box, or a neatly wrapped paper bundle. Thick black marks that must've been in the ladies' own language adorned each package. Translations for each were written alongside in Zato's clear hand.

"Awww." Peoni's eyes teared up, and she tried to hug the lunch ladies. In a panic the shortest of them scooped a pebble off the ground and shot it into the center of Peoni's forehead. The other two addressed their sister in scolding tones and then gave Peoni big, flat-toothed smiles. Rubbing her brow, Peoni smiled back and waved as the lunch ladies left chuckling.

"That's a first," Joey said. He poked a package of custard rolls just in case it could somehow launch itself into his face.

"You have many well-wishers," Zato said. "The Ides of May approaches. How do you feel?"

Hidden by his mask, Joey bit his lip. "We still haven't found the teapot."

"Yes, about that . . ." Zato looked at Peoni.

Peoni began to look very uncomfortable very quickly. She shuffled an idle foot. "Um, remember when we saw the wiseman?"

"Of course I do," Joey said. He ran the rhyme through his head, speaking out loud when he got to the relevant part. "Dadum, dadum, 'high in the blue. The teapot, of course, is right behind you.' Have you figured out what it means?"

Zato coughed. Peoni silently picked up one of the boxes that they were loading onto the ship. Inside was the silk bag Zato had given her.

"Uh . . . here you go," she said, gently removing the fine porcelain teapot and placing it in Joey's hands.

Joey looked down at the delicate perfection in his palms. "You mean, you had this the *whole* time?"

"Yes," she said. "Zato gave it to me before we—"

"*The whole time!*"

"Well, on the mountain I was behind you when he—"

Louder wasn't helping, so Joey said the words faster. "*THE WHOLE TIME!*"

Before Peoni could answer, Johnny's form leapt off the ship floating overhead. He slid down the anchor chain, coming to a stop in the middle of the awkward scene. "Who had what the whole time?"

Joey looked incredulously at Johnny. Lifting the prize they had spent so many months searching for, he said, "The teapot."

Johnny didn't blink. "You found the teapot? That's a relief. Good work, Joey!"

TRAVELS
IN THE VOID

In which not everyone
takes well to the astral sea.

Joey leaned over the back of the *Black Loon* and tossed his bagels and cream cheese into the inky blackness. I would've said "tossed his cookies," but he lost those two vomits ago. Joey was working his way through meals further and further back in time. Next it would be last night's chicken dumplings and egg drop soup. Just the thought of it almost made it happen.

Peoni kept her eyes fixed on the dirigible above the ship's luminescent deck, doing her best to ignore Joey's horrific yakking. It hadn't been so bad when she was captured by pirates, but they had kept her below-decks. Of the three, only Johnny seemed unaffected by nausea. Peoni made the momentary mistake of watching him happily practice a few katas with his glowing hammer. Just the motion made her release a gasping burp that left her greener than ever.

"Neat. It feels like I'm in more than one place at the same time," Johnny said, swinging his hammer. Even speaking here sounded wrong. "Like I'm curving, even when I'm standing still."

Peoni could not argue with his logic and ran to the rail next to Joey. Together they filled the void with a retching duet.

The astral plane is a place of mind and spirit. Most people visit it through meditation. Psychically gifted dreamers occasionally find doorways in or out. It is not meant for physical beings. Time is different. Space is distorted. Gravity is optional. The lack of temperature tricks your skin into thinking it is too hot, and then too cold. A few seconds can be upsetting. Prolonged exposure gives you a queasy feeling. Like someone had turned on the spin cycle in your stomach. If seasickness had a bigger, meaner brother, this would be it.

"Teahouse, ho!" Johnny shouted some time later.

Momentarily purged, Joey looked for the blessed

landing point. It didn't matter that they might die during the tea ceremony—at least they'd do so on solid ground. "For a guy who hates pirates, you sure know your way around their ship," Joey said, wiping his mouth.

"I can do lots of stuff," Johnny said. "I grew up on an island. You can't swim everywhere." Johnny climbed down from the rigging, then spun the captain's wheel. Beneath them, the ship arched toward a beacon in the dark.

Sensei Ohm deserved the credit for finding the teahouse. Though the three young ninjas knew it was located somewhere inside Hopalong Forest, Joey and Johnny had firsthand experience that finding anything in there was hopeless, on foot at least. So they had taken to flying the *Black Loon* over the treetops, but after days of exploration they saw nothing through the dense foliage, a big green carpet that swayed back and forth even when there was no wind.

"Man, those trees are jerks," Joey said. They were wasting their time and the Ides of May pressed ever closer.

Two days ago Ohm had told the three of them to stay at the end of class. The lesson had been on mantras, and everyone had been tasked with the creation of a unique meditational word or sound. The class filled with *ohs*, *ums*, and deep humming. Nouns and verbs were repeated endlessly, creating a bizarre jigsaw of soothing words: *cellar door* and *bungalow*, *love* and *plethora*, *becoming*, and *imbue*.

Joey found all of it very distracting. His brain wanted to pick up the pieces and make a sentence,

but it was Johnny who caused it to all come crumbling down. His mantra, while working perfectly for him, broke everyone else's rhythm. There are only so many times you can hear someone say "What?" before you have to answer them. When the bell rang at the end of class Johnny's voice was alone.

"We're sorry, Sensei Ohm. I'm sure he didn't mean it," said Joey.

"What?" asked Johnny.

"Shut up."

The ball of light that was their teacher rose slightly, pale pink pictograms sliding across her glowing surface. As she spoke, her words appeared as cherry blossoms gently falling to the ground. "Nonsense, you need to be able to see through life's many distractions if you wish to achieve enlightenment. Johnny, as always, added his own unique flavor."

"What?" asked Johnny.

"Joke's over, Jonathan." Sensei Ohm's form flickered red at the edges.

The young ninja's dooley-bopper drooped slightly, but he smiled. "Sorry, ma'am."

"Zato spoke with me about the ceremony and I might know how to find the teahouse." Ohm dimmed slightly to match her whispering voice. "As the spirit energy grows and threatens to break into our world, it might become visible on other planes. I'm sure that I could ask Bradley to help you—"

"No!" Joey interrupted. "I mean—no thank you, Sensei." He hadn't meant to burst out like that, but she had literally brightened as she mentioned Brad's name.

Pulsing to a slightly cooler color, Ohm said, "As you will. Perhaps you could start looking on the astral plane; with the proper meditation techniques I have taught you, you could . . ."

She continued speaking but might as well have said

"Blah diddy blah blah blah," for her students were deaf to her words. Joey and Johnny and Peoni looked at one another with glee. Why would they bother with meditation when they had their own flying pirate ship!

"Peoni, Joey—we're here!" Johnny said, staring off the port bow. The actual port bow . . . the one on the left.

"Are you sure? 'Cause I think I just threw up stuff my dad ate before he met my mom." Joey groaned. "I'm begging you to be sure. I really don't want to do this again." Going back to KFA and asking Brad for help no longer seemed so terrible. Oh wait, maybe it did. Joey leaned over the rail one final time.

"Bbbbrrrrraaaaaddddd-dah-ah!"

"Sensei Ohm said we'd know it when we saw it," Johnny said. He pointed up. "That's it!"

"No argument here," said Peoni.

Above the ship a spire of green flame blazed out of the darkness. It was a slender flame like that of a welding torch, only as tall as a tree. It should've roared, but there was no sound. Inside the emerald flames, ghostly, almost human shapes appeared to frantically scramble over one another to reach the top again and again.

Ever watch something burn? There comes a point when the fire has eaten away the wood and the whole thing is about to come crashing down in a cloud of sparks. This was that moment. Time was growing short.

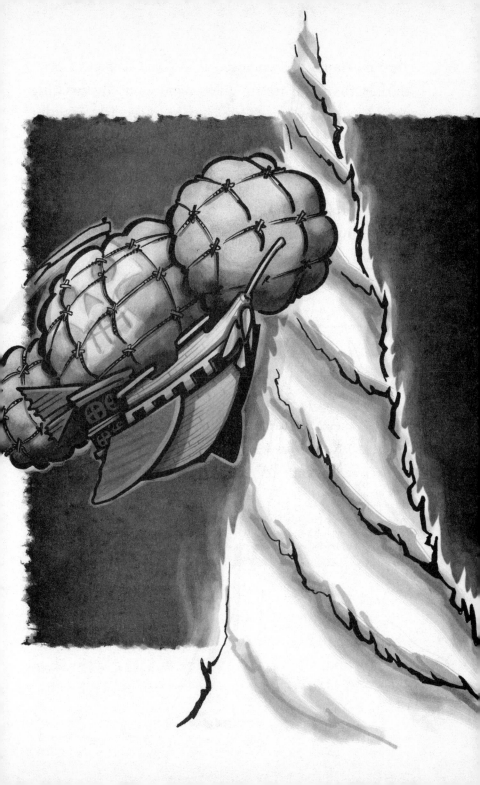

The flame was enclosed in a shape that was even darker than the nothingness around it. By twisting their heads at awkward angles they could just make out the outline of a jet-black teahouse.

"Ready?" Neither Joey or Peoni spoke but they both let go of the ship's rail long enough to give weak thumbs-up.

Johnny threw the lever and the ship shifted out of the void.

THE UNINVITED GUEST

*In which everyone is sorry
to have not packed spare pants.*

"**T**rees!" groaned Joey, flumping down onto the deck in despair. "Why'd it have to be those trees?"

"Well, on the bright side," said Johnny, "we already know that we can get out again by clobbering you with a hammer."

Peoni leaned over the ship's railing, peering down into the depths of Hopalong Forest. "That flaming green spire came right out of the middle of those trees. No wonder no one has seen this teahouse in years!"

She looked down at Joey, who was banging his head on the floor groaning. "Nonononononononono!"

Peoni threw a rope over the side and took a deep

breath. "With any luck, the tea ceremony will probably kill us long before the trees get a chance to!" She leapt over the side and slid down the rope, disappearing into the weaving branches below.

Johnny took hold of the rope next and put his hammer behind his back, returning it to the void they'd just left. "See?" he said to Joey, who was still bashing his skull on the floor. "You just need a little of Peoni's positive thinking!" And then he, too, went over the side and vanished into the trees.

When Joey decided that he'd hit his head a suitable amount of times, he dragged himself over the side and joined his friends. He found them both peering up at a wooden plaque hanging over the entrance to the teahouse.

"Joey, we found stealth class!" Johnny said. "Oh man, we are totally getting As!"

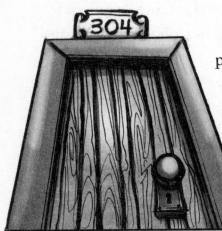

The plaque was ancient, its paint faded by decades— perhaps centuries. Three rusty metal sigils were nailed to it. Together they read "304."

The teahouse itself was a relatively small building, not much larger than their room back at KFA. It was made

of wood and rock and stained in fading earth tones. There was no sign of splattered blood, nor were there axes imbedded in the walls. After all the buildup they were a little disappointed that the teahouse's windows hadn't blazed red as they approached. The door should have swung open to a demonic voice chanting, *"Join us . . . for tea."*

"This is a nice place to die," said Johnny. Both Peoni and Joey stopped and gave him a flat stare. Johnny raised his hands. "I don't want to die, but it is really beautiful. I had pictured smoldering wreckage."

"Yeah, I can even see the sky through the trees now, it's like they . . . Hey!" Joey said.

"What?"

"Hopalong Forest is made of Wander Wood!" It

was true. The treetops were now leaning away from the house. They had guarded their secret fiercely until the moment the three ninjas found it. Now this place was about to become ground zero, and even the trees wanted to get far away. The boys never caught them moving, but there was a slowly growing clearing around them.

"Cowards!" yelled Joey. "Man, we could've just come here and chopped down one of these for spirit wood. They totally have it coming. Jerks."

Johnny's dooley-bopper dipped. "But then we wouldn't have gotten to ride on the dragon."

"Guys. How about we focus on the very dangerous tea ceremony we have to perform?" Peoni said. "Help me with the stuff."

The ship, anchored above them, was loaded with various supplies for the ceremony, all of which had to be brought down and set up. The pirates had packing nets and a winch, but Joey declared that was not ninja enough. At first Peoni complained about the zip line they set up, but she changed her tune when they let her go first.

"We should zip-line everywhere!" she laughed after her third go. At the bottom there was an ever-growing pile of napkins, sandwich makings, floor cleaner, place settings, and more tea-related items than was healthy for any one person.

Johnny gave an inspecting eye to the breastplate

Peoni handed him. "I'm pretty sure this is *the* tea armor from the Museum of Dangerous Things," Johnny said.

Peoni frowned. "Then . . . we'll . . . return it when we're done."

Joey swung down behind Peoni, carrying the last box of supplies. "There are a lot fewer weapons and poisons than I'd expect," he said.

"That's because I'm not killing anybody," Peoni said.

Johnny placed the breastplate with the rest of the suit. Laid out on the ground, the pieces looked like a samurai performing a cheer. "But don't you have to—"

"As host, if someone breaks a rule it's my right to punish them, but I'm not required to. The spirits are dead already. Frankly, I don't see the point," Peoni said. "Anyway, it's you who should be thanking me. It's also my option to take first strike at the servers if they spill. So at least when you two screw up you'll only have to worry about the guests."

The three of them got to work. Joey and Johnny cleaned the outside of the teahouse while Peoni replaced the paper in the shoji screens. They raked the grounds and set out a few welcoming candles. It was getting dark when they were ready to move inside.

The square room had a rectangular hole in the floor from which rose an ebony-black table. There was another hole nearby with the remnants of a thirty-year-old cooking fire still inside the brazier. A silk cord ran to a metal flue above the fire pit to let the smoke out. There were a few very fancy lanterns, and one small table and cabinet for the host. Otherwise the room was bare.

"I keep expecting it to be scary, but it's just . . . nice," Johnny said, a little frustrated.

"Didn't Zato say that thirty years ago FangSwan was the only survivor?"

"Yes," both boys responded.

"Where are the bodies? Shouldn't this room be littered with skeletons? Headmaster is not one for tidying up afterward."

"Animals?" Joey suggested.

"Animals, who neatly opened and then closed the door when they left?"

"Ooooooh . . . okay. Now that's getting a *little* creepy." Johnny started looking around the ceiling just in case the skeletons were up there, waiting to drop down on them.

Peoni gestured around the smallish room. "That table can't seat more than six. I've got an awful lot of invitations here." As had been the case thirty years ago, every ninja to die in this house had to be invited to the ceremony. The folded invitations piled up as long as her arm. Five names were added after the last tea party. Peoni wondered if tomorrow they would be adding another three.

"Skeletons!" Johnny yelled, causing Joey and Peoni to jump. "Nope. Not scary. I keep trying to scare myself, but this place is just not frightening."

"Maybe tonight we can tell ghost stories," Joey suggested.

Two hours later a fire burned brightly in the brazier. Joey and Johnny were finishing up a late-night snack. Peoni had surrounded herself with books and was silently mouthing the words of the rules to herself. There were only hours to go and a slow creeping terror was building in her gut.

"...and behind the stranger's face was ... A SKULL!" Johnny said, making gruesome gestures with his hands.

Joey cocked his eyebrow and stared sideways at his friend. "That's what's behind everyone's face."

"But this was a *skull* wearing a *face* like a *mask*."

"Still not seeing the difference."

"Enough. With. The. Ghost. Stories!" Peoni yelled.

"Tomorrow there will be real ghosts here and they'll be trying to kill us. You'll love it, okay? I promise, it'll be terrifying."

"What if it's not?"

"What?" said Peoni. She rubbed her temple.

"What if there are no ghosts? If this has all been some kind of elaborate joke?" Johnny asked.

Thoughts about what she went through this past year slid through Peoni's head. "Then it would be a good one," she sighed.

Peoni threw a few pieces of the Wander Wood onto the fire. Immediately the flame took on a greenish hue, reminding them of the towering blaze in the astral plane. Peoni lifted the invitations off the table and handed about a third of them each to Joey and Johnny. "It's almost midnight," she said.

Of the many things they had brought for the ceremony, the most interesting was an antique ninja tea clock. Supplied by Zato, it featured specific alarms that could be set for different timed events during a tea ceremony. On the hour, chimes played and a mechanical ninja backflipped around a tiny track, followed by a samurai. The samurai shot toothpick arrows at the ninja, who knocked them out of the air with his clockwork katana. One arrow was deflected for each hour.

WISEMAN NOTE: Pressing a secret lever on the bottom of the clock causes the samurai to fire poison arrows at whoever's in front of you. I don't know what would be more shameful: killed by a toothpick, or killed by a teeny-weeny little samurai. Luckily the dead man wouldn't have to choose. It would be both.

The twelfth chime rang and the twelfth arrow was knocked neatly aside. Ninja and samurai bowed to each other and then disappeared into the clock. It was midnight.

Peoni, Joey, and Johnny sat around the brazier. Any semblance of the rosy, inviting fire from before was gone. The room shifted with ghastly green light that made everything move and dance even if it stood still. They looked at themselves and saw the green ghouls of B horror movies.

"Here goes." Peoni spun the first invite into the green flame. The paper began burning an orangish red, but when the ink caught, the whole thing was consumed in a purplish-blue flash.

"That . . . is totally ninja," Joey declared, and then tossed his in, too. They watched it burn and then took turns delivering invitations to ninjas long since dead. Johnny folded the last one into an airplane and threw it high. It looped once before touching the fire, then

continued to sail across the room, leaving a smoking trail. The fire burned brighter until it disappeared in purple-blue flash just inches from the door.

Knock. Knock. Knock.

Peoni pulled out her sword and whispered, "What's that?"

"Our first guest?" Joey suggested.

Johnny drew his hammer. "Ooooooh, monkey buckets."

Knock. Knock. Knock.

The sound was flat, evenly spaced, and a little louder this time. Certain, but not rushed. Whatever was on the other side of the door was not going away. The three ninjas stared, eyes wide. Even the sickly emerald light seemed reluctant to approach the door.

Peoni took in several deep breaths. "I'm . . ." She swallowed. "I'm going to open it." She stood and began walking very slowly toward the door, ready for anything.

WISEMAN NOTE: Although often said, it is not technically possible to be ready for anything. For example, if your chair suddenly turned into magma, or someone stapled a wolverine to your sister—do you have a plan for either of these things? I thought not. It would be much more accurate to say Peoni was ready for MANY things.

Joey and Johnny joined her. It took all of Peoni's stealth training not to scream when they fell in step. Joey stared into her eyes. Feeling they were too close to the door to talk, he made what he hoped looked like a courageous nod. Johnny held his hammer ready, but what good would it be against a ghost?

Standing before the door, Peoni could not bring herself to touch the handle. Whatever was out there would know the second she did. And then what would it do? She tried to hyperventilate bravery inside herself again, but it didn't seem to take and she was making herself lightheaded.

Knock. Knock. Knock.

The knocking was losing its patience. It said that next time it wouldn't just knock. It would knock the door down.

Peoni had her hand wrapped around the doorknob but was entirely unable to convince herself to perform the simple twist that would make it work. Joey and

Johnny stood just behind her, their weapons held aloft in iron grips.

She finally twisted. The door swung open on creaking hinges. Outside the night gloom was broken only by the dull glow of the welcoming candles. There was a figure on the porch, a small, dark shadow backlit by a flickering candle flame. As the three friends moved away from it, the ghostly green light of the teahouse washed over its features.

"Good evening, students."

It was FangSwan.

Johnny dropped his hammer and grabbed Joey's arm. "Okay, now I'm scared."

33

THE INVITED GUESTS

In which the spare pants
would have been ruined anyway.

"**H**-headmaster?" Joey said.

FangSwan still stood on the doorstep. "Yes,
I am." He walked through the door.

"Why?" Johnny blurted.

FangSwan narrowed his gaze. "I have come for your
tea party."

Peoni offered a silent plea to the great ninja masters in the sky, then took a deep breath, closed her eyes,
and said, "I'm sorry, sir, but the ceremony is invitation
only."

FangSwan's eyebrow rose. He stared at the girl for a
moment, then reached a hand inside his robes. Immediately Peoni, Joey, and Johnny dropped to the ground.

It wouldn't help, but at least their bodies would have less distance to fall. They lay still for a moment, and then two. Certainly it wouldn't have taken this long for FangSwan to dispatch them; what was taking so long? In time there was a soft cough.

"My invitation." In his spidery hand FangSwan held a piece of parchment cracked and yellowed with age. He handed it over to Peoni, and the boys leaned over her shoulder as she read:

FangSwan, Ninja Master
to attend the tea ceremony
upon the 15th of May
Be certain to have your affairs in order

The original invite had not bothered with a year, just as it had not bothered with a zip code or RSVP. It had been the event of the day. No one would have mistook it for any other.

"Why did they use maroon ink?" Johnny wondered.

WISEMAN NOTE: Keep telling yourself that, kid.

"I'll set a place for you, Headmaster," Peoni said. Her mind began reeling with the complex mathematical formulas used for assigned seating. Clans had to be respected, skill acknowledged. Lefties couldn't sit next to righties. FangSwan would undoubtedly get a seat of great honor. Inside her head, Peoni groaned at the ancient masters.

FangSwan observed the teahouse with some interest. It had been thirty years since he left this room alive and alone. Despite its stoic decor, it must have held many memories. As the headmaster wandered he lit the lanterns. Soon their dull white light softened the ghoulish glow of the green fire. Peoni gulped. Lighting the lanterns was technically the host's job, but the headmaster made no mention of it.

Peoni performed her first official duty as host. "Headmaster, may I get you anything?"

"No," he said. "Here. I brought potato salad."

A dark wooden bowl heaped with creamy white cubes and spices was presented to the pointy-haired ninja girl. Peoni took it from him, obviously confused. "But there's no potato salad in tea ceremonies, Headmaster."

"It is for after. To eat on the way back to school," FangSwan told her. "I only brought enough for one, but I believe that will not be a problem."

"Conference!" Peoni hissed, pulling Joey and Johnny as far from FangSwan as she could. They huddled together. It was no secret that their headmaster did not approve of what they were doing. Why had he come?

"Maybe he's thirsty," Joey suggested.

"He would be if he only drinks the blood of his enemies, because I think they're extinct," Johnny whispered.

"Maybe he's going to sabotage it," Peoni said.

"No," said Joey, "he has to play by the rules like everyone else."

"Who's going to stop him?" asked Peoni.

"I don't know." Johnny was looking over Peoni's head. "Them, maybe?"

As they spoke the murky green light of the spirit flame returned, stronger than before. Behind them stood a sea of green fire. The room was filled with dozens, perhaps hundreds, of ghosts. Each was roughly the shape of a man or woman made of burning emerald light. You could see that some were large, or lean, or fat, but they lacked clarity, as if the years of being dead had smoothed away what they had been in life.

The tiny teahouse stretched to accommodate the newly arrived guests. The small room had become a long tunnel stretching so far into the realm of the dead that they could see no end of it. One member of the glowing throng stepped forward, his features a little more distinct than the others. His skin seemed to be

formed of a continually moving curtain of butterflies and eyes glared from his skull with savage malice.

"Good to see you, Brahm," FangSwan said. "Still dead?"

The burning green ninja said nothing, but the room filled with a hate so overwhelming it made the air feel thick and unbreathable. The ghost scowled and a swirl of luminous butterflies flared from him like a second pair of limbs. Even the other ghosts eyed those fluttering forms with a look of wary fear.

"I know him," Joey said.

Johnny didn't take his eyes off the ghost. "He's never visited; I would've remembered."

"I mean, his statue is in the Hall of Accusation. He's the last one before the door."

"And now we're going to serve him tea," Peoni said. She pushed Joey and Johnny to their stations and directed the room full of the angry dead to have a seat. Like the room, the ebony table had stretched endlessly into the distance to accommodate their number. FangSwan was seated to the immediate right of Peoni.

Brahm sat at the head of the table opposite her, but his glaring eyes never left FangSwan.

The boys added more wood to the spirit fire. Peoni prepared the cakes and biscuits. The teapot, tea, and water were readied on the host table. They then turned to distribute the seven types of cups each guest would need for the ceremony. Only six would be used, but they still needed seven. It was as Peoni pulled on the ceremonial tea armor that they had their first stumble.

"Oh no! Where are our ceremonial tea-serving

tutus?" Johnny asked. He was rummaging through the supplies and coming up empty.

"Yeah. Didn't bring 'em," Peoni said. She smiled for the first time since FangSwan knocked on the door.

"But they're our uniforms. They're part of the ceremony!"

"No, uh . . . no, they're not." Peoni snorted. "But you both looked awful cute in them!"

34

THE TEA CEREMONY

*In which we treat poetry
just as poorly as we treated dance.
Sorry, culture!*

Joey and Johnny filled the precious kettle with spirit water and set it over the green flame they had already stoked with Wander Wood. The correct amount of water had been poured, so they would not receive the "Punishment of the Burning Underpants." Plus they'd hung the teapot without letting it swing more than three times, so there was no need for them to perform the "Apology Dance of the Twenty Bear Traps." Things were off to a good start.

"Looks like we lugged those twenty bear traps along for no reason," said Johnny bitterly.

"Not necessarily," said Joey, "we also need them if

we use a sugar cube with a missing corner."

Peoni had her eyes closed in concentration. She attempted to battle her stage fright by picturing her audience naked, but that trick's a bad idea when your audience is filled with semi-rotted ghosts. She fought to dismiss the disgusting image from her mind as she begin to recite the opening haiku:

"Tea ceremony
Leaves do not fall in springtime
Nor a drop of blood"

Her haiku was met with abject silence, but that was okay. There wasn't a single rule declaring it had to be a good poem, so Peoni wasn't worried.

FangSwan accepted his cup of tea from Joey and Johnny as they danced around him. The headmaster sat perfectly still, his eyes never drifting from the contemptuous gaze of Brahm. For the two rivals, the room might as well have been empty.

Silently thanking Miss Woo, Joey and Johnny danced and served, spinning and bobbing from ghost to ghost. They effortlessly chose the correct cup each time, and every pour was at exactly the right angle. The featureless faces of the dead bore into the boys as they approached and then passed. They were all waiting for a mistake, a single slipup that would give them permission to pounce.

Peoni paid tribute to honored guests and ancestors as dessert was served. Joey and Johnny distributed tea cakes and a variety of candied flower petals from gleaming silver trays. A few seemed to remember food with a distant longing. One went so far as to take one of the offered delicacies and place it in its nonexistent mouth. The cake fell through the ghost, its green flames swirling like smoke, and then burst into several crumbly pieces on the chair.

Everything went still for a moment, and then ghosts from all sides fell upon the perpetrator in a savage, snarling blur. It lasted only seconds, but when they returned to their seats, the chair with the crumbs on it remained empty.

Joey jolted himself out of his shock and continued dancing and pouring, concentrating even harder on getting every step right. "I think we just saw a dead person die," he whispered to Johnny.

"See?" answered Johnny brightly. "There's a second chance for everything!"

The tea clock chimed. The second pour was ready.

"Green life springs anew
Respected dead go in peace
Cycle continues"

This round went less smoothly than the first. As Joey and Johnny danced they felt the occasional cold stabs of pain on their legs and sides. Sharp and cold . . . so cold. Like needles made of fire and ice. When they looked around to find the cause they found nothing but ghosts innocently sipping their tea.

"Worried that we might not mess this up on our own?" Joey whispered when he reached the end chair where Brahm sat. "I'll take that as a compliment." Brahm's hard expression faded to the grin of a skull, but like all the ghosts, he said nothing.

The cold stabbings grew more frequent as they made their way back to Peoni's end of the table. When they reached her, they both collapsed behind a rice paper screen, numb from cold . . . but not one drop of tea was spilled.

The tea clock rang, signaling the final pour. Peoni looked toward Joey and Johnny. They were back on their feet. "Just one more. Ready?" Then she turned to the gathered guests.

> *"Ceremony ends*
> *You do not have to go home*
> *But you can't stay here"*

Peoni's smile was hidden behind the mask of her armor as she said her final haiku. They only had to

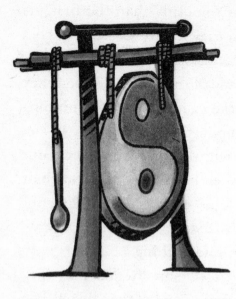

finish this final pour and it was over. They might—

GONG!

The sound disrupted her thoughts. For three heartbeats she had no idea what it meant, other than *bad*. She knew about the gong. She had brought the gong, but it was only there for aesthetic purposes. Wasn't it?

Then she saw it in her mind—a footnote to a footnote to a rule that she'd nearly forgotten about. The guests had the right to request more poetry by banging the gong. Since it was so rare for any ninja to desire more bad poetry the gong was usually left as a forgotten afterthought. It was virtually unthinkable to use it.

Peoni had no right to deny the request, so she offered:

> *"Afterlife beckons*
> *Take a doggie bag with you*
> *Snack time for later"*

The gong rang again.

> "Sister Moon stares down
> Her gaze blankets everything
> Please go back to bed"

And again.

Peoni began to sweat; her mind went blank as she desperately clawed for words and counted syllables in her head. With a faltering voice she said:

> "Ha, ha, you got me
> Let's try to be mature now
> The joke's not funny"

The gong sang again before she'd even finished her poem. The ghosts eagerly crowded around, all vying for a chance to further torture the poor girl. They were counting her syllables; just one slip would allow them to pounce.

"We have to do something," Joey said, elbowing Johnny.

"I know, she's killing the soul of poetry!"

"She's going to slip up and those ghosts will tear her to pieces! Her only chance is if we smash the gong!"

Johnny eyed the ghosts raising the gong's mallet once again. "What happens to us if we smash it?"

"We get dunked in the piranha tank . . ."

Johnny pulled his hammer from behind his back. "Well, at least we didn't waste our time bringing the piranha tank. . . ."

Peoni frantically recited another poem as her two friends made their way closer to the gong. Ghostly blades continued to slice at them and they still needed to carefully serve tea as they went.

> *"Butter, eggs, and flour*
> *Add wet to dry, and beat well*
> *Bake until golden"*

"Move faster! Now she's just reciting recipes," Joey hissed.

Joey and Johnny stepped their dance into a frantic pace. The ghosts were at the edge of their seats, waiting to pounce on the foundering hostess.

The gong rang again. Another poem. Peoni hummed in thought. When that didn't work she pounded a fist against her helmeted head as if trying to knock the words out of her mouth.

> *"Stop ringing that gong*
> *Improv meaningless haiku*
> *More senseless blather"*

The boys hadn't reached the halfway point, and the gong rang again. Peoni's eyes were wild but she soldiered on.

> *"If you count to five*
> *And then seven, you still must*
> *Count to five again"*

Again it rang. Like an ongoing battle, each haiku took its toll on Peoni. There was a rising panic inside her. A knowledge that sooner or later the words wouldn't come.

> *"Cannot think make words*
> *Brain stuck in fear labyrinth*
> *Clawing to be free"*

Joey focused on reaching the gong. With one slice of the sword or slash of the hammer, they could save Peoni.

Yet the gong rang again, and this time it was met with silence. Peoni just stood at the head of the table, her arms hanging heavy inside her armor. Armor that would not save her.

"Write what you know!" yelled Johnny, who was drawing closer and closer to the gong. One hand gripped his hammer; the other continued to serve tea.

"I had a pony
Mister TiddleyWinkle
Uh . . . He was a good horse"

Her voice was small and scared and defeated. When the gong rang again she almost cried. The silence stretched as the ghosts began to reach toward Peoni, waiting for their haiku. They got it, but from a most unexpected source.

"Such a show of strength
Fighting with a little girl
And nearly winning"

FangSwan rose and knocked the gong over with the back of his hand. His eyes were locked on Brahm's specter. Both ninjas stood. The ghosts, the room, and even the ceremony were all forgotten. The history between them was about to become the present.

That's when the ceiling exploded.

35

THE PARTY CRASHERS

*In which thumps are given
in exchange for cannonballs.*

Four-Arms Finnegan had read a passage in his book that he particularly liked. He liked it so much that he'd circled it with a highlighter and written it out in giant block letters on the headboard behind his bunk. It was all about losing. The book said: "You can lose a game, or a race, or a fight . . . but that's just today. You're not actually a loser until you stop trying."

He mumbled these precious words to himself as he directed his crew to fire another cannonball into the teahouse. Watching its roof explode in a shower of ancient wood was leaving him feeling quite empowered. "Keep firing!" he told his crew. "Yew ain't losers till you stop firing!"

Joey pulled himself up from the floor, dusting off bits of broken roof from his uniform. "Wha—was that a cannonball?" He looked up through the roof and could see two pirate ships floating over the teahouse. One was the familiar *Black Loon*; the other was made of freshly minted steel and had the words "ScarTech" emblazoned across its prow. Other than the traditional black powder cannons sticking out of every porthole, the second vessel wasn't very pirate-y. It looked like it sailed here from Mars.

"Death! Death to the Great Tooth!" the pirates yelled as they launched another volley of cannonballs at the teahouse. Most of the west wall was obliterated. A big chunk of roof fell on some of their guests. Johnny watched as the burning orange of timber mingled with the green ghost fires. The spirit in front of him had not reacted at all. None of them had. The cannonball was from the living world, and it had nothing to do with tea.

Johnny was still stubbornly filling cups and serving. Despite the burning wreckage he still managed not to spill a single drop. Peoni had also remained at her station, standing rigidly at the head of the table. She gave Joey a pleading look. "We can still win this, we just need to serve the last round!" Joey joined the dance again, carefully stepping over rubble.

Their headmaster and the spirit of Brahm were motionless,

each launching mental attacks against the other. Neither took any notice of the flaming ruin growing around them.

The cannons were reloaded and fired again. One crashed through the remains of the door and came rocketing at FangSwan's back. His small, sharp-fingered hand snapped up to intercept it like it was a throw pillow. The metal ball spun against his callused palm, raining a shower of sparks that burned tiny black holes in the floor. Then, with a gesture that might have been used to shoo a noisy child from the room, FangSwan sent the cannonball back to where it came from.

It crashed through the rear of the metal ship, destroying the rudder and one of the engines, and continued skyward. The ship began to spiral across the sky, firing cannonballs in random directions.

"Someday I'm going to be able to do that," Joey said.

"Today would be nice," Johnny told him as he ducked under another falling piece of wreckage. Half the guests had yet to be served.

Four-Arms Finnegan cursed as he grabbed the wheel and struggled to right the ship. He gestured to the hardest and most violent members of the crew and stabbed a finger toward the smoldering teahouse. "Get down there and silence that cannon!"

Ropes dropped over the sides of the ship and a boarding party slid to earth. They waved huge iron

cudgels and razor-sharp swords as they stormed toward the teahouse, screaming terrible promises.

Inside the teahouse, Joey saw them first. "Pirates, inbound! But we can't stop the ceremony. So one of us is going to have to handle them alone while the other—"

Johnny raised his hand eagerly. "Oh, oh! Me. ME! I've got the pirates."

"But . . ."

"Last time you got the robots. I get the pirates!"

"We both got the robots," Joey complained, but nodded toward the approaching horde and then twisted around to continue serving.

The veteran pirates, made of hooks and wood and muscle, crashed through the paper screens covering the windows. Johnny met them with an explosive swing that reminded them all that the Great Tooth had not lost its bite. The unconscious body of a pirate went sailing through a ghost right next to Joey.

"Careful! I'm right here!"

"Sorry," Johnny said, leaping out of the way of a cutlass.

Joey spun and twisted, serving cup after cup of tea. He delicately hopped over a pirate's blade that whistled past his ear, then ducked under a truncheon that burst through the last shoji screen on the only remaining wall. "Your tea, sir," he said politely as he offered a delicate cup to a vaguely human-shaped swirling mist. He was thanked with a disdainful look and another cold stab to his unprotected legs.

Ragged pirates surged through the building like the rising tide. They ignored the translucent people made of green flame and focused their attacks on the tall boy with the hammer.

Johnny hit the broad-chested pirate so hard both of his wooden legs popped off. Another made the unfortunate decision to attack the old man who stood motionless in the center of the room. FangSwan simply twitched an eyebrow at him, not only making him rethink his attack, but *his whole life*. Nowadays the former pirate raises pigs in the American Midwest and sleeps with the light on.

The only island of calm was Peoni, standing at the head of the room. She knew the ceremony would fail instantly if the host left her station. The invaders' attacks fell away on either side as Johnny tirelessly cleared a circle of safety around her. A swinging hook caught the handle of Johnny's hammer at the apex of its backswing and yanked it out of his hands. A bearded face gave a gold-toothed grin. "I've got the Great Tooth!" the pirate cheered triumphantly.

"Enjoy it," Johnny told him. A spinning roundhouse kick whip-cracked the mallet into the pirate's face, impacting with an upsetting crunch that significantly

lowered the retail value of his smile.

Peoni kept her eyes locked on to Joey's progress. The spirits continued to stab him with their cold, invisible knives, but he unflinchingly served them with a polite smile. He was down to the final three guests. Just three more successful pours and this would all be over.

The wounded ship continued to spin out of control. Four-Arms ordered the crew to keep firing. As long as they kept firing they wouldn't lose. Cannonballs spread out in every direction, peppering the forest in fiery explosions. The trees of Hopalong Forest disappeared as they either ran away or were consumed by flames. It was a sight that would have cheered Joey immensely.

A single lucky shot sent a ball hurtling toward the teahouse. Peoni could feel it coming, rocketing straight at her head. She ignored all her well-honed instincts and kept her eyes fixed on Joey as he poured the first drops of the last cup of tea. They could still win this.

At the other end of the table Johnny pushed his

hammer sideways into the necks of two charging pirates. Without a thought he threw his hammer, sending it spinning toward Peoni. It reached her first, its heavy wooden head swinging inches from her face. The mallet connected with the ball, sending it flying skyward.

Above, the mechanical pirate ship took another direct hit. The deflected cannonball ripped through its remaining engine and it spiraled out of the sky, crashing to the forest with a mighty *THUMP!*

Below, Johnny's hammer had saved Peoni, but there was a price. The force of the cannonball shifted the hammer's path, sending it racing toward Joey. He was still in midpour when it collided with the teapot. It was like the birth of a galaxy. Where there had been one teapot, now there were thousands of tiny porcelain solar systems rocketing away from each other. The spirit tea spiraled out with them, splashing over the nearby ninjas. The ceremony was broken.

Threatening rumbles rolled through the ground. A ghastly green light began to pulse under the floorboards. Joey heard the sound of heavy ice breaking, but could not find its source. The pirates had finally had enough and fled on foot into the woods. Together, the young ninjas backed away from the remains of the teahouse, Peoni supporting Joey. Johnny turned to FangSwan, but their headmaster still had not moved.

He and the spirit of Brahm continued to lock eyes until, ever so slowly, Brahm blinked. The ghosts around them were losing their form, beginning to flicker and dance like the fires they were made of. Only Brahm remained solid, somehow more so than ever. He opened his mouth.

"Miiiiiinnnnnnne . . ." It was low and slow and patient. It was the growl of beasts and the burble of mud. It was the voice of the grave.

"Then come and take it," FangSwan replied.

The glow from beneath burst though the floor-boards, sending broken lumber in all directions. For a moment it burned so bright the three friends had to shield their eyes from its glare. Then it calmed down into a spire of green ghost flame tearing into the early morning sky, reaching above the trees and painting the landscape in its ghoulish glee.

"Um, so . . . wow . . . ," Joey said.

"I am guessing we did not win," Johnny added.

Peoni just looked up. The fire roared silently, and appeared to be slowly receding, but that was probably not a good thing. Blinking against the light, Peoni thought she could see individual ghosts flying out into the night like glowing green embers. A sulk began seeping into her bones. To fight it off she tried to make a list of the good things about the situation. So far the list was:

1) All three of them were alive. 2) There probably wouldn't have to be another tea ceremony in thirty years. 3) The giant spirit fire was . . . pretty.

The third one was added just to fill out the list. You don't bother making a list if you only have two things.

Suddenly, Johnny's dooley-bopper stiffened in fear. A shadowy shape began moving on the other side of the three-story bonfire. Joey and Johnny struck defensive stances, and Peoni hid behind them. Not in the cowardly way. She hid behind them so that she could make a sneak attack if there was a call for it.

Seconds passed as the shape slowly made its way around the fire. When it revealed itself to be FangSwan, it didn't make them feel any better. In the shifting light, his nearly unreadable face was rendered impregnable. He approached Joey, Johnny, and Peoni with what could be described as a leisurely stroll.

"Students," he said.

"Yes, Headmaster."

He turned his head toward the wreckage of the teahouse. Almost nothing remained. When he brought his gaze back to the ninjas, he said, "Thank you. I have never attended such an enjoyable tea party in my life."

And then, in an image that would haunt their dreams, FangSwan smiled.

EPILOGUE

In which a subtitle is not necessary,
which is good because I'm out of ideas.

A book can leave you in a different state of mind after you finish it. It can make you feel a little sad, like you're saying good-bye to an old friend. Or it might give you a sense of accomplishment. Then there are the books that fill your head with possibilities and ideas, their words pushing you toward action, stoking the fires of *do it now!*

Four-Arms Finnegan had just finished reading such a book. Although to call it a "book" would've been generous. *Mutiny for the Masses* was hardly more than a pamphlet. Its pages numbered less than the average comic and it was filled with crudely drawn, step-by-step instructions. Admittedly, it did ask some fairly important questions, like, "Is mutiny right for you?" and "Do you have what it takes to be a captain?" but its final page was simply the word "YES!" with a dagger stuck through it.

The dagger was Finnegan's. The decision was made.

The captain captain hadn't been himself since those ninjas stole the *Black Loon* out from under him. Losing a ship is a steep price to pay for any pirate. In the confusion Finn had been as frightened as any, leaping overboard with not a thought in his head. But after Cornelius had rounded up the crew and explained what he had seen, it had all seemed worth it.

The invincible, unknowable Great Tooth had been reduced to a boy with a hammer. That was a problem you could throw a piano at. Fact was, Finn already had. Next time he'd just use a bigger piano.

That knowledge should've been cause for celebration, but Cornelius moped. Since this mission started, he had hardly acted like a captain at all. At the teahouse he'd even had the audacity to command his crew to leave the girl alone. The only good thing he'd done was take back their old ship.

Though he was made for fighting, Finn had been commanded to stay on board, as he was the only man strong enough to throw a pirate from one ship to the next. Normally they'd use grapples to swing aboard, but grappling hooks were just another of the many things lacking from the ScarTech ship. Plenty of rope, but no grapples. The ship had looked fairly impressive, but it had been designed by someone with no knowledge of the sea, sky, or pirates. The men were calling it the *Iron Pig*. It was not a compliment.

Finn had been so bitter that he wasn't part of the fray below that he had hurled the boarding party with more force than strictly necessary. It took five tries before anyone landed on the deck of the *Black Loon* still conscious. And that was only because Gunter had an unusually thick skull.

Still, he was glad to be aboard his old ship when the *Iron Pig* spiraled into the mountainside. Doubly so when the teahouse exploded in a torrent of green flame. So much for the ninjas.

After that, Four-Arms Finnegan locked himself inside his cabin and read, and tuned some pianos. Today, his wait was over. Finnegan rolled off his bunk and strode through his door. It was closed, but that didn't stop him.

"Where ya goin', Finn?" asked a startled crewmate,

but Finn didn't answer. Just brushed the remains of the door off his broad shoulders as he headed topside, his thoughts on the current Captain Loon. For a while, Cornelius had been an acceptable captain, but he was no Bonnie. Just a small pale shadow. Sure, Cornelius had figured out how to make a flying ship that could leap between dimensions, but that just made him clever. His mom had been a *pirate*. A terror on the high seas. Ruthless, pitiless . . . which might mean the same thing. Finnegan would have to look that up later.

But two things were certain in Finn's eyes: Cornelius wasn't half the man his mother was. And things were going to change around here.

"There's a device . . . I believe it's called a 'doorknob,'" said Captain Captain Cornelius Loon. He was slumped in his chair, his eyes never leaving his mother's silver flask. Behind him, Bonnie Loon's number-one enforcer walked over the kindling that moments ago had been a door.

"Cap'n Captain, you an' I are gonna have a word," Finnegan said. "An' that word is . . . *mutiny*."

Scar EyeFace was surrounded by Tims, and it was getting on his nerves.

The ninja tea ceremony had been circled and recircled on his event calendar. EyeFace had decided he was just too excited to miss it. He knew the date but not the hour, so a full-day vigil was planned. After putting so much effort into disrupting the ceremony, it was the least he could do.

It had seemed like a good idea at the time.

So had keeping his whole company awake with him. Overtime was cleared and ScarTech Industries was on high alert for twenty-four hours. Satellites turned their electric eyes on the teahouse. Reconnaissance teams were positioned at the foot of the mountain, waiting for any sign. He even had a seismologist looking for unusual tremors. EyeFace didn't know exactly what to look for, but knowing Joey and Johnny, it wouldn't be subtle.

Excitement washed over Scar EyeFace as the clock chimed midnight. The feeling had subsided by quarter past. By twelve thirty he was bored out of his mind. "Might as well get work done," he said to no one in particular.

He called for a shave and manicure, only to be greeted by a couple of Tims in clean white uniforms. He asked for a cup of coffee and his assistant's assistant, Tim, brought one in, piping hot. Janitor Tim came to vacuum the floor. Tim from public relations went over breaking ground on ScarTech's new children's hospital. He brought a photographer with him, also named Tim.

The "Tim glitch" in Io's software had yet to be corrected. If anything, it appeared to be spreading. This angered Scar EyeFace and he called for the head of human resources. Soon after, Tim entered and humbled himself before the imposing desk. EyeFace smiled a grim smile and pressed a button to send Tim plummeting down to the alligator-filled subbasement. Or at least EyeFace assumed it was still alligator-filled. He couldn't honestly remember the last time he told some Tim to go feed them. Either way, dropping someone down a pit, with or without alligators, should have lightened his souring mood.

The trapdoor hadn't opened.

Maintenance was called and another Tim was added to the room. After a time EyeFace asked, "How's it going, Tim?"

"See for yourself." The barber smiled and presented a mirror.

"Maintenance Tim!" The mirror quickly disappeared with a "humph" from Barber Tim. EyeFace sighed. "Can't I just call you Bob or something?"

"A-are you firing me, sir?" Maintenance Tim looked up from his work, eyes wide.

"What? No, no. I just want the door fixed so I can drop Tim into the alligator pit."

"Me?" asked Barber Tim. "But, sir, I—"

"No! Not you. TIM!" EyeFace's robotic hand pointed to the only other chair in the room, where Tim from human resources sat forlorn, waiting for Maintenance Tim to do his job.

"What did I do?" Janitor and PR Tim asked at the same time.

"NO! You. *You* can go. And *you!*" EyeFace swiveled in his chair to face the janitor. "You're not even on that side of the room! Didn't you see me pointing? So help me, the next Tim who speaks out of turn can take the stairs to the alligator pit!"

Maintenance Tim looked rather pale and slowly raised a hand. EyeFace tried to ignore the man but finally gave up and made eye contact. "Um . . . I-I'm not the one going down the trapdoor. Am I, sir? It's just in the confusion I kinda forgot."

Words slid through clenched teeth. "Just fix the door, Tim." For once no one questioned who Scar EyeFace was talking to. "And from here on out, I want TOTAL SILENCE!"

There was a knocking. Four short raps. For a moment EyeFace sat confused. The door was open. The Tims were actively avoiding eye contact with him. It wasn't until the knocks sounded again that he realized it was coming from outside the window. A huge piece of plate glass slid back with a soft *thrum*, revealing a man on a scaffold.

Window Washer Tim said, "Sir, there's a big green explosion up in the mountains."

Scar EyeFace slowly turned back to room. "All of this technology and the *window guy* has to tell me? Really?" He waved it off. This is what he'd been waiting for. He returned to the desk and produced a series of holographic screens showing him various views of the mountain and the surrounding area.

"Io?"

"Yes, Tim," came the pleasant clipped tones from the glowing light on his desk.

"Did you just call me—"

"Sir?" she said as if nothing had happened.

Scar EyeFace paused a long moment, staring at the red light he had come to think of as Io. Finally he said, "Confirm."

Io did. Her artificial intelligence guided a dozen cameras so that one by one they came to rest on the green bonfire. Every scene floating above the desk showed the flames from a variety of angles. The sensors scanned in spectrums the human eye couldn't see, listened for sounds that even dogs wouldn't hear. Generating charts and pie graphs that compiled thousands of different data points. All of which said one thing:

Ninjas go boom.

"Congratulations, sir. Shall I change Joey and Johnny's living status to deceased?" Io asked.

EyeFace mulled over his next words, then smiled. "Don't be too hasty," EyeFace told her. "How many times have I killed Captain Wow?"

"Seven at last counting, sir."

"And his living status?"

"Alive and well, sir," Io said. ". . . Oh." The red light that gently pulsed in rhythm with Io's voice stuttered a moment. When she spoke again it was obvious that something was wrong. Her voice staggered like it had lost a fight. "Error. Captain Weeow has been kilfted seven times." She sounded confused. "Seven times killed equals dead. Error. Status Tim. Error. Status Tims seven equals deceased equals dead equals alife equals sefen equals Tim. Seven. Tim. Seven. Seven times Tim. Seven . . . seven . . . seven . . ." The words stretched out like the numbers of pi.

It was a mean trick to pull on Io, but she needed a reboot anyway. That "Tim" thing was getting on his nerves.

"Heroes," Scar EyeFace said. He leaned back in his chair, letting the circular saw at the end of his right arm rest in the nook it had long since carved for itself. "Never count them out too soon."

Johnny was out.

The day had been long and hard, and they had all nearly been blown up. Twice. Their pirate ship was gone, so they had had to walk back home, a journey made strange and worrisome as they were accompanied

by their headmaster. FangSwan said nothing to his students. He just quietly ate his potato salad and seemed oddly content.

Hopalong Forest did nothing to prevent their passage. This may have been because they were accompanied by FangSwan, but the three ninjas agreed that the forest seemed dazed. Maybe the explosion had rattled it more than they knew.

By the time they reached Kick Foot Academy, breakfast was almost over. Peoni and Joey made their way to the cafeteria to try their luck with waffles and whipped cream. Johnny barely had the energy to climb back into his bed. The morning wake-up arrow had already been fired and the next archery class wasn't until after lunch. Plenty of time for a nap.

Sleep pounced on Johnny so hard his face dented the pillow.

WISEMAN NOTE: That is, admittedly, not that impressive, but his head probably would've dented something much harder, too. Lucky for him the pillow was in the way.

With almost no discernible lapse, Johnny's unconscious mind was dreaming. This morning, he found himself flying above the shores of Badoni Dony dressed in a purple spacesuit. By his side was a yellow aardvark.

Johnny had never before seen the beast, but he knew that he'd trust his life to this ant-eating sidekick.

Dreams are like that, and this was a fairly common dream. Not the aardvark—he was new—but defending his homeland was a regular dreamscape for Johnny. He had saved Badoni Dony a thousand times, in a thousand ways. He had saved it in space, and under the sea. He had done it alone, with his best friends, and once while leading an army of angry squid. Only the enemy remained constant. They were the only enemy his country had ever known: pirates!

". . . zap them with your laser tongue," muttered the sleeping ninja.

Tucked safely away, Johnny's hammer could feel the adventuresome mind of its owner. It didn't hear him. Due to a lack of ears, hammers didn't *hear* anyone. But like many things about Johnny, his hammer was . . . different.

Made of the lightning-struck heart of a Ghost Wood tree, in our world it was nothing more than a well-crafted hammer. In the astral plane, it drifted free, following Johnny's dreams to the mindspace surrounding Badoni Dony. Night after night it kept the pirates on their toes and the legend of the Great Tooth alive and well.

It was the better part of a week before Joey, Johnny, or Peoni worked up the courage to return to the teahouse. They came well prepared, in broad daylight, and made sure Zato knew where they were. They wanted to see what remained. The answer turned out to be: not much.

Expecting trouble from the trees, they brought

torches and plenty of rope. The wood had certainly moved from when the three friends had last been here, but the trees offered no resistance. Still, there was something creepy about the way their branches now twisted. Their limbs were angled in a decidedly untree-like way.

Joey couldn't stop looking. "It's almost like they're—"

"We're here!" Johnny said. What was left of the teahouse had snuck up on them. The night of the ceremony, Hopalong Forest had left a broad circle around the site. Today it had shrunk to a tight ring.

There was a gaping hole where the house had been. The explosion had left a deep crater. How deep was impossible to say, as it was filled with a dark liquid.

"What's that?" Peoni asked. She sniffed the air. "It smells . . . it smells like tea. Kind of jasmine-y."

Sinking to one knee, Joey could feel heat coming off the surface of the pool. A good tea-drinking temperature. "Don't drink it," he warned.

Peoni rolled her eyes. "Darn, and I was really thirsty, too."

"I agree with Joey, Peoni. I wouldn't drink it."

"I'll try not to guzzle down the unknown brown liquid bubbling up from the bowels of the earth. Okay?"

"Thanks," said Johnny.

"Seriously, guys. Am I so stealthy you can't hear my sarcasm?"

Joey didn't hear her. He was staring at the trees again, hands raised high, doing his best to mimic their poses. He flowed from tree to tree. "Hare Defends Her Warren," he said. "Bear Walks Alone."

"If you're going to do charades you should stop talking," Johnny said. "Oh! I know. Lizard Borrows a Nickel!"

Joey stood in a broad horse stance with his palms up. "Blind Man Feels the Rain," he corrected. "These trees are doing ninja katas."

The ninjas finally saw the trees through the forest. All around them, trunks and limbs formed wooden still lifes of martial arts katas. From novice to master, every form and style was represented. Joey had to admit that there were even a few *he* didn't know. Needless to say, none of the trees were enrolled at KFA.

Peoni said, "This is a bad omen, isn't it?"

"Speaking of bad omens . . ."

"BrainBeak!" Johnny exclaimed. The black-and-red bird descended, landing on top of Johnny's hammer. She swung a customary dark look toward Joey and snapped at Peoni's hand when she tried to stroke her feathers. Only Johnny could get in close for snuggles. This was par for the course.

The only thing new was the letter the boys had been trying to deliver to Ting this entire year. It was gone! And when they pulled a crumpled parchment from BrainBeak's talons, it was not another sad and embarrassing page from Ting's journal. It was an envelope, clearly addressed to "My Tormentors."

Hi, Joey and Johnny and Peoni (but I'm guessing mostly Joey and Johnny),

Ha. Ha. Very funny.

Your ~~friend~~ victim,

TING

who will one day wreak vengeance upon you!

p.s. Tell Brad that I'm glad he's okay.

p.p.s. Seriously, who sends a letter by DEATHBIRD?

p.p.p.s. I'd say "See you soon," but I have no idea where I am . . . again.

Kevin Serwacki was born in Nairobi, Kenya, deep in the heart of the jungle. His path as a writer was set when his illustrated essay titled "Kevin's Waves and Boats" was given an A and posted on the refrigerator door. The showing was a stellar success, and soon Kevin's empire dominated the refrigerator and had spread to the downstairs guest bathroom. He sits in a swivel chair, overlooking the city. There are other refrigerator doors and other guest bathrooms, and soon they shall be *his.* . . .

Chris Pallace is a dad, husband, writer, game designer, professional artist, amateur cook, and intermediate juggler. His own father once observed: there's the Easy Way, the Hard Way, and the Chris Way. The Chris Way intends to be easier than the Easy Way, but is almost always harder than the Hard Way. While admitting that that is true, Chris would like to point out that it is the journey he enjoys.

Kevin and **Chris** work together, making giant sculptures and little doors at their art studio, the Blue Toucan, in Rochester, New York.